QUANTUM LEAP

OTHER TITLES PUBLISHED BY BOXTREE

QUANTUM LEAP

THE BEGINNING

JULIE ROBITAILLE

BOXTREE

Quantum Leap: The Beginning, a novel by Julie Robitaille, based on the Universal television series QUANTUM LEAP, created by Donald P. Bellisario. Adapted from the episode 'Quantum Leap', written by Donald P. Bellisario.

First published in Great Britain in 1990 by Corgi Books.
Published in 1994 by Boxtree Limited, Broadwall House,
21 Broadwall, London SE1 9PL

Copyright © 1990 by MCA Publishing Rights,
a Division of MCA, Inc.

All rights reserved

3 5 7 9 10 8 6 4

ISBN: 1 85283 392 0

Except in the United States of America this book is sold subject to the condition that it shall not, by way of trade or otherwise, be lent, resold, hired out or otherwise circulated without the publisher's prior consent in any form of binding or cover than that in which it is published and without a similar condition including this condition being imposed upon a subsequent purchaser

Cover artwork by Keith Fowles

Printed and bound in Great Britain by
Cox & Wyman Ltd., Reading, Berkshire

A CIP catalogue entry for this book is available from the
British Library

PROLOGUE

I was having the most extraordinary dream. It had all those wondrous childhood fantasies of flying in it, but it was somehow . . . different. This wasn't that kind of smooth, safe flight over pastoral fields and bustling cities; this was no magic carpet ride full of giddy whirling and breathless expectation. This was more a jet-like rush, a weightless ascension, arrow like, through roiling, threatening clouds in bruised purples and blacks, with thunder and lightning splitting the sky. This was up and up and up, and then, just as suddenly, a dead rock plummet down and down to an earth rising towards me at frightening speed.

I gasped as an immense Boom! startled me awake. My eyes popped wide open as the last sonic reverberation died away. It was early, close to dawn, and there was just enough light filtering into the room for me to see. I turned my head to check the time.

I blinked, then blinked again. I was looking at something utterly unfamiliar, something from another time, another place. It appeared to be a bulky tube-type clock radio that told the time with numbers that turned on rolodex cards. As I stared, bewildered, the cards flipped from 4:59 to 5:00. I heard a click.

'Well, since my baby left me . . .'

Elvis? I thought. An Oldies station? I don't listen to Oldies stations, not unless I'm stuck in traffic. An Oldies station on an oldies radio?

'I found a new place to dwell . . .'

I shrugged mentally. Oh, well, so it was a multi-part dream. I closed my eyes and waited to see what would happen next – dancing cobras, space ships, Sonia Braga. But nothing happened. Nothing, that is, that was very dream-like. I could smell a freshly washed pillow case, and I could still hear Elvis, but otherwise . . . I opened my eyes again and lifted my head.

It was a bedroom, all right, but like the clock, I had never seen it before. Yellow curtains with a strange, Mondrian-like geometric print covered the windows. The walls were a plain, flat beige, unrelieved by any kind of picture or decoration. I peered down toward the foot of the bed, past the bump of my feet sticking up under a light plaid blanket: there was a somber mahogany foot-board, partially blocking a matching dresser. On the floor, against the wall nearest me, I could see a blue trunk with the letters U.S.A.F. stencilled on the lid. If this was a dream, I thought, it was weird in the weirdest way . . . So uneventful. So banal. Well, I thought, give it another try, maybe it will get better. I closed my eyes again.

Right about then I became aware of something else. Something rustling in the bed. Something warm, some-thing next to me. No, I thought, don't panic, just keep your eyes closed, keep them . . . I felt flesh brush up against my thigh.

'Jesus!' I leaped up and rolled out of bed, my feet making unexpectedly real contact with a cool linoleum floor.

'What's the matter, Tom?' Who? The voice seemed real. Sleepy. Female.

I turned, slowly, cautiously, to face the speaker. It was a yawning woman, a woman with blonde hair, sitting up on the other side of the bed. She turned and looked at me, her sleepy blue eyes crinkled against the morning light. She smiled. A familiar, happy smile.

'Bad dreams, honey?'

I just stared, my mouth open.

'Tom?' she said, a puzzled look creeping over her fresh face. 'Are you okay?'

I just nodded speechlessly.

She smiled again. 'I'll go put the coffee on,' she said, and heaved herself up. Under pale blue baby doll pajamas, an abdomen that looked to be about six months pregnant protruded. The woman shuffled across the linoleum yawning. She paused, kissed me lightly on the cheek, and then continued on out the door.

I simply stood there, frozen to the floor, my heart going triple time. I was standing in a bedroom I'd never seen before. With a pregnant young woman I'd never seen before. This wasn't my house. Tom wasn't my name. And this wasn't a dream.

CHAPTER ONE

Take a deep breath, I told myself. Count to ten. Visualize a placid lake . . .

None of it worked. The feeling of utter disorientation didn't go away. Where was I? Who was I? What the hell was going on? After a few completely unrewarding moments of trying to figure out the answers to those questions, I forced myself to leave the bedroom. I crept down a tiny hallway and guessed right: the bathroom. Relieved, I shut the door behind me and sank down on the toilet to think the Situation over. The Situation, with a capital S. I tried to remain calm and collected.

Okay, I knew I wasn't dreaming and I knew I wasn't Tom. That was all very well and good, but it didn't do much to help the Situation, because the plain truth was, I didn't know who I *was*. And there probably isn't anything more panic producing than not knowing who you are. I fought the feeling – panic wasn't going to help. Clear, rational thought, I told myself firmly.

Let's see, I mused, it could be, uh, temporary global amnesia. Now where had that phrase come from? I brought my hand up to my head and felt my skull, running my fingers through thick short hair. There didn't seem to be any bumps or other evidence of a crack on the head. Could you get amnesia some other way? My mind was a blank on that one – then again, if I didn't know my own name, could I trust myself to think that medical diagnoses were my strong point?

Maybe this was all some kind of hallucination. Caused

by . . . hmmm. Caused by . . . food poisoning, that must be it! Mushrooms or bad sushi or something. Only, I didn't feel sick, and besides, I couldn't remember what I had eaten the night before. I couldn't even remember *if* I had eaten. Bottom line, I admitted grimly to myself, was that I couldn't remember the night before at all. Jesus, I thought, this was getting worse, not better.

'Tom, honey,' the pregnant blonde's voice drifted sweetly through the closed door, 'they were out of your regular shaving cream at the PX again, so I got you some of that, you know . . . what's it called? The one that you see on the cute little billboards all along the highway?'

PX, I thought: that plus the stencilled trunk, I'm in the Air Force? And billboards, what billboards? I stood up and opened the door to the medicine cabinet above the sink, hoping to find something there that would give me information, give me a clue.

It was filled with vaguely familiar objects. Familiar, but somehow, wrong. Ipana toothpaste, with Bucky Beaver – how did I know that name? – grinning from the front of the tube. An aluminum double sided injector blade and an old-fashioned shaving brush and mug. A small glass bottle of Merthiolate. Another of Calomine lotion. No safety caps, no plastic. A tube of diaphragm jelly, dusty from disuse. I remembered the blonde's advanced pregnancy – at least *this* made sense. Of a sort, anyway.

And a can of Burma Shave, that stuff on the cute little billboards along the highway. Except that suddenly, somehow, I knew that Burma Shave was something that hadn't been sold for years. And years. What kind of colossal joke was this – that had to be it, a *joke* – and who was playing it on me?

I reached for the can of shaving cream and turned it around and around, looking, I suppose, for some sort of proof, or a clue. Something that would confirm that this was a fake, a prop in an elaborate hoax. But the can appeared to be brand new and perfectly real.

The door to the bathroom flew open and the blonde stared at me in surprise. 'Why haven't you showered? You're going to be late. Here.' She held out a fork for me, and I obediently bit a piece of sausage off the end of it. It tasted real. She smiled when she saw what I was holding. 'Burma Shave, that's it.'

She brushed by me and reached past the gaily printed plastic shower curtain, flicking on water. 'Come on, Tom, get in,' she urged me.

What was I supposed to do? Zombie like, I walked into the shower and heard a peel of laughter from the woman.

'Oh, Tom,' she said, 'sometimes you are just too much.'

As the water cascaded down my back, I looked down and realized I was still holding the Burma Shave can. And I was still wearing my skivvies. Whoever she is, I thought, she's right. Sometimes I'm just too much. I heard the bathroom door shut behind her.

Okay, I thought, as the water poured over me, let's try sensory perceptions first. I already knew my taste buds were working. I fiddled with the water. Scalding discomfort was followed by a rash of goose bumps: so hot was still hot, cold was still cold. But what did that prove? I shook the can of Burma Shave and squeezed a mound of white cream into my hand. I smelled it. Uh-huh, the old nose seemed to be in working order, too. Again, so what? So my skin and my nose and my mouth were all functioning – what about my brain? I shrugged helplessly, at a loss, then stepped out of the shower, and wiped away the steam cloud on the mirror.

'Aah!' I jumped back a foot and plastered myself against the opposite wall, in an abbreviated, terrified retreat from the stranger who stared back at me from the looking glass.

'What's wrong?' The door flew open and the blonde hurried in again. 'Tom, what's *wrong*?' she repeated anxiously.

I pointed at my reflection. *Not* my reflection, that is – the person staring back at me had dark hair, a chiseled young face, and a terrified expression. *That* part was right, anyway. 'What . . . what do you see there?'

'What are you talking about?' Her eyes were wide and worried.

'*There!*' I pointed again. 'Who is that?'

All of a sudden she sighed, all the confusion draining from her pert face. 'Honestly, Tom, sometimes you just don't know when to stop kidding. What do you want to do, scare me into early labor?'

'I'm serious,' I insisted, 'who do you see in the mirror?'

She shook her head indulgently and looked. 'You,' she said. 'My husband, Tom Stratton.'

Tom Stratton, I thought, who's *that*?

She came up beside me, and ignoring the dripping skivvies, put her arms around my shoulders. We both stared at the couple reflected back at us, she blissfully unaware that one half of the couple had no recollection of his own name or past, their meeting, marriage or . . . I looked at her swollen belly . . . mating. Her blue eyes crinkled again. 'And his very stretched-out wife, Peg.'

Peg, I thought, what an old-fashioned name.

Peg turned around and examined herself critically in the mirror. 'God,' she said ruefully, 'I look terrible. I've been rubbing that cactus juice . . .'

'Aloe vera,' I said automatically.

'Is *that* what it's called?' Peg said. 'Anyway, I've been putting it on my stretch marks, but I don't think it's really doing any good.' She glanced up mischievously at me. 'Will you still love me when I've got hideous white stripes?'

'Huh?' I was still trying to figure out where the words aloe vera had sprung from.

'Tom!' she said reprovingly. 'Here I am talking about you and me and love and looking like an albino zebra, and all you can say is huh?'

'Not exactly,' I said cautiously. 'Ah . . . my name's not Tom.'

'Here I am looking for a little reassurance that . . . what do you *mean*, your name's not Tom?'

'Uh, Peg,' I began, her name feeling alien on my lips.

'*What?*' she said challengingly. 'What is going on with you, Tom?'

Before I could fashion a sane reply – presuming I *could* – we were interrupted by another voice.

'Daddy!'

A small boy in bright pajamas flew around the corner and looked up expectantly at me. 'Daddy, Captain Birdell's on the phone.'

Oh, my God, I thought, I'm a *father*, too!

Peg's blue eyes were studying me, beginning to get serious again. 'Tom, honey,' she said, 'are you feeling sick?'

'Uh . . .'

'Because if you are, no excuses, you aren't going to fly – it's not safe.'

'Fly?' I said blankly.

Peg turned to the little boy, who hovered in the bathroom vibrating with kid agitation. 'Mikey,' she said, 'go tell Captain Birdell that daddy will call him back when he gets out of the shower.'

Mikey's eyes widened. 'Daddy's already dripping wet,' he observed.

'Ah, well, yes. He is,' Peg agreed hurriedly. 'You're

absolutely right about that. Now go on, before Captain Birdell hangs up.'

Mikey saluted. 'Roger, over and out,' he said, and raced off.

'And get his number, write it on the pad by the telephone,' she called after him. She turned back to me. 'Just in case he didn't sleep at the B.O.Q.,' she grinned, 'which he doesn't seem to do half the time.'

I had absolutely no idea who or what she was talking about. But something Peg had said had tapped into a heretofore unreachable void. My mind, up until this moment, a wondrous and terrifying blank, suddenly spit forth a random piece of information.

'555-2231!'

'What?' Peg said.

'The number,' I said excitedly, 'I know the number!' I felt like letting out a whoop of triumph. 'Excuse me,' I said to Peg, who looked confused. I brushed rapidly by her and followed the little boy into the living room, leaving a wet trail in my wake.

Mikey was still holding the receiver, and I grabbed it unceremoniously from his little hand. 'Sorry,' I said, punching my finger down.

'Ouch!' I picked it up again and shook it. There were no buttons on this black relic: a rotary dial, clumsy and cartoonish, offered up a slow circle of numbers.

'What's the matter, Daddy?' asked Mikey. 'Why'd you hit the phone?'

'Mistake,' I said hastily. Out of the corner of my eye, I saw Peg move into the room, her belly swaying. She clasped her hands comfortably across it and stood watching, as I waited an interminable amount of time, first for a dial tone, then, as each number took its slow trip up to the marker and back.

'555-2231,' I muttered under my breath. '555-2231.'

It was the first tangible memory I had, and I didn't want to lose it.

'What are you doing?' Peg asked curiously.

'Calling the office,' I said matter of factly.

'The office?' Peg said dubiously.

I nodded happily, drumming my fingers on the cherry-wood tier-table that held the phone.

A rapid, piercing 'beep-beep-beep' suddenly emanated from the receiver, and I yanked it away from my ear. 'What the . . .' I promptly began to re-dial.

'Blockfield eight, four, seven.'

'Huh?'

Peg repeated, 'Blockfield eight, four, seven.'

'Beep-beep-beep,' the receiver shrieked again.

'What the hell is wrong with the phone?' I said, frustrated.

'There's nothing wrong with the phone, Tom, you're just dialing too many numbers,' Peg said.

'That's impossible,' I said impatiently. Then an idea struck me. 'Not *enough* numbers, that must be it, I didn't dial the . . . what's the area code here, anyway?'

'The what?'

'The area code,' I repeated.

Two sets of puzzled eyes met mine.

'What's an area code?' asked Peg.

'Like a secret code?' Mikey interjected excitedly. 'Gee, Daddy, how would we know? You *never* tell us the secret codes!'

'What could possibly be secret about an area code?' I asked them, but their expressions were as confused as mine must have been. 'Never mind,' I shrugged, and dialed 'O.'

'Hello, this is Operator 23,' said a polite, disembodied voice. 'How may I help you?'

Well, I could think of more than one reply to *that*

loaded question – like do you happen to know my name, or where I am, or how I got here? An answer to any of the above questions will be greatly appreciated. But I contented myself with asking, 'Can you tell me the area code I'm calling from?'

There was a blank pause on the other end of the line. 'I'm afraid I don't understand, sir, would you mind repeating the question?'

'The area code,' I repeated apprehensively.

'I'm sorry, sir, I'm afraid I don't know what you're talking about.'

The operator's genuine bewilderment convinced me. 'Thank you,' I said dully, and hung the receiver up, defeated. As I did, I saw the numbers on the front of the phone I was using: Blockfield 621. Peg hadn't been kidding. She gave me a peculiar glance, then shrugged.

'If this is another one of your silly practical jokes,' she said, heading for the stove, 'this is not the time or place. You haven't eaten, and Bill's going to be here any minute.' She began heaping pancakes and sausage on yellow Melmac plates.

I looked around the room, really looked, and suddenly I felt a little tremor of apprehensive understanding. No, I thought, that's ridiculous. I kept looking. From the low-slung Danish modern couch and coffee table to the pink and black formica dinette set, with its boomerang design dancing across its top; from the black and white Motorola television with its distinct oval screen to the parchment shaded matching lamps, their vaguely bowling-pin shaped ceramic bases decorated with geometric slashes and triangles; from the pregnant blonde with the poodle cut wearing frilly pastel baby dolls to the quizzical looking little boy in Davy Crockett pajamas . . . this entire scene was like a flashback to someone else's life. The key words being flashback, and someone *else*.

Mikey's eyes followed the path mine took, then looked directly at me, as if for reassurance. I didn't have any to give him. It couldn't be. No way. These things didn't happen. Still, I walked hypnotically through the front door and out onto the street. I had to see if my vague, growing suspicions could possibly be grounded in fact.

It was an ordinary enough street. The sun was shining, birds were singing, the neighborhood was coming awake. Neat, nearly identical houses, gleaming cars and carelessly tiptilted tricycles lying in driveways – nothing ominous about that, just the ordinary suburban stuff. Ordinary enough, that is, when houses had flat roofs featuring old-fashioned t.v. antennas and evaporative coolers; when roads were gravel instead of blacktop; when the car in my driveway – *Tom's* driveway – was a pristine, new, '55 Chevy sedan, and every other car on the street was of the same vintage.

I stood there, stunned in the morning light. In the distance, beyond the houses, dusty desert stretched for miles. I could just make out the towers and hangars of a small airbase, and the dry lakebed it abutted. Behind the airbase, purple mountains, emerging from the morning shadows, gave a surreal perspective to an already surreal scene.

I heard the whistle of a jet overhead, and watched, transfixed, as it came in for a landing. It was close enough for me to see that it was old and bulky, as outmoded as the clock radio and everything else I'd seen since I opened my eyes. An F-80 Shooting Star. A fighter plane that had been used in the Korean War. And not since.

From the open doorway of the house that was Tom's, I heard the faint strains of Peg and Doris Day singing 'Que Sera, Sera.'

You got it, Doris, I thought grimly, whatever will be will certainly be. I wondered fleetingly what would happen if I just gave up, walked in the house, phoned for an ambulance, and told the men in the white coats to come on down to the Twilight Zone and get me.

But then, it didn't seem like much of an option when I thought about the vintage of everything around me – cars, clothes, music. Because in the 50s, I seemed somehow to know, the only kind of treatment they regularly prescribed for crazy people consisted of the stuff of horror movies – electroshock therapy.

And although I was pretty certain that there must be some sort of rational explanation for what was happening to me, convincing a bunch of shrinks would be uphill work. I had heard somewhere that shrinks ask you three initial questions to check your sanity. Your name. The name of the President. And the date. And I had the distinct feeling that I would flunk all three.

CHAPTER TWO

A child's voice broke my reverie. 'Daddy, Captain Birdell just called again! He said to tell you he'll be here in ten minutes, and mommy says that you'd better hurry up and get dressed.'

I turned to face the unfamiliar suburban house with its unfamiliar suburban inhabitants, and saw Mikey – right, Mikey – hopping around in the open doorway. He was certainly a cute enough kid, with his open, winsome face and his Davy Crockett p.j.s, but he wasn't *my* kid.

'Come *on*, Daddy,' he said impatiently, 'come inside, you look like such a *cootie* standing out there in the street like that.'

A cootie? I glanced down and thought that I probably looked more like a confused pervert, in my wet underwear and undoubtedly bewildered expression; but I got the message. Time to go in. Time to get dressed. Time to start the day. But whose day was I starting?

I walked slowly back into the house, trying to gauge my plan of attack. It's a difficult task, when you don't know who you are or where you are, to even attempt to formulate any kind of plan, but one thing was clear. I had only two choices in this nightmarish situation: confess that I had no idea who or where I was and take the consequences, or try to play along, fake it, get some information, and figure things out for myself. Tom's self. Whosoever self. Jesus, I was getting confused just trying to sort that part of it out – the second was still the better of the two choices, I thought.

Inside the cheery, out-of-time house, Peg was rinsing the dishes. She looked over her shoulder as I came in. 'You really shouldn't walk outside like that, honey,' she said in a gently reproving voice. 'What will the neighbors think?'

'You're right,' I agreed humbly. 'I seem to have gotten off on the wrong foot this morning.'

'You *do* seem a little distracted,' Peg agreed. 'Probably just a bad dream you don't remember or something.'

'Uh-huh.' I stood there, unsure what to do next.

'I laid your clothes out,' Peg said.

Whew. 'Thanks, honey,' I replied, and headed for the bedroom.

'Wait a second, mister,' Peg said.

Uh-oh, I thought, she's figured it out.

'Don't I get a kiss?'

'Of course,' I said, relieved. I changed direction and gave her a light peck on the cheek.

'Is that the best you can do?' Her merry eyes twinkled.

It certainly *was* – I felt strange enough just doing that. But I just grinned and shrugged and said, 'Well, honey, I guess it's like you said, I'm distracted this morning.'

Peg stood up on tiptoes and kissed me on the mouth. She tasted like coffee and orange juice. 'There, isn't that better?' she asked.

'Much,' I said. Then I fled.

'Tom,' Peg called after me.

'What?' I hovered in the little hallway, certain that every sentence was the start of discovery.

'Don't forget to shave.'

'Right,' I said, and turned automatically into the bathroom.

I made a mess of shaving. I was used to an electric razor, and the archaic injector blade looked and felt clumsy in my hand. Which was nothing compared to how my face looked after it was applied. Which was *still* nothing compared to shaving a stranger's face, every line and stubble an unfamiliar one. I swore to myself as I rummaged around in the drawer beside the sink and finally came up with a styptic pencil, which I applied generously to that now raw, strange face. After that, there was nothing to do but put those little bits of torn up Kleenex on the worst of the cuts and go get dressed.

Inside the bedroom, the bed was already made up, a white chenille spread neatly pulled over the plaid blanket. The print curtains were pulled back to reveal the driveway, and beyond it, the row of identical houses; beyond them, there was a different view of the mountains, now fading from purple to a dull, pale brownish color.

I turned my attention to the task at hand. On the bed lay a khaki Air Force flight suit with silver Captain's bars on the shoulder. I'm Tom Stratton, Captain Tom Stratton, I told myself as I pulled it on. And the uniform looked nice and tidy and kind of jaunty in a retro sort of way on whoever Tom Stratton was.

It had to have been coincidence, but the bulky tube radio which Peg had left playing – I supposed Tom Stratton liked to get dressed to music – chose that moment to break into the Platters' rendition of 'The Great Pretender'. Uh-huh, there I was, and that was exactly what I was going to have to do, be the great pretender, until I could figure out exactly what had happened to me.

Maybe, I reflected, as I tried on the aviator sunglasses and tried to angle the peaked barrack's cap just right on springy dark hair, this was all something that had been done to me – a kind of experiment. A . . . psychological experiment? Maybe . . . hypnosis? Hmm, hypnosis. That could actually make a certain kind of sense, I thought.

I played with the idea of hypnosis for a moment, and finally came up with a plausible theory: I was in some sort of scientific experiment, and I'd been given post-hypnotic suggestion. For some reason which I would learn when I came out of the trance I was in, I had been hypnotized to wake up this morning and believe that it was 1956, and I was an Air Force captain named Tom Stratton with a wife named Peg, a son named Mikey, and a baby on the way. Maybe it was some sort of stress test or . . . I ran out of theory here.

Well, even if I *didn't* know the why of it, it still wasn't a bad explanation for the Situation. So all I had to do to keep my sanity, I told myself, was just play along with things until my subconscious got the signal – the snap of the fingers or the next sonic boom or the right song on the radio – to come out of it.

Just at that moment, there was the sound of a car horn blasting practically right outside my window. Ah-ha! I thought, relieved that it was finally going to be over. The sound of a horn – this is it! I waited with excitement to *really* wake up, for my memory to come flooding back. But nothing happened. The horn sounded again.

'Tom, honey, Bill's here!'

It was still Peg's voice. It was still 1956. And I – Tom – was still about to go off to work. My shoulders sagged under their flight suit. Then I straightened them up again and told myself to keep on going. Well, I thought, giving my unfamiliar reflection one last glance in the mirror, hi-ho, dude. And good luck.

I sped through the living room getting a quick 'bye' thrown at me from Mikey, who was planted in front of the Motorola watching Clarabelle cavort on Howdy Doody; and I managed to make it out the door blowing an air kiss to Peg, and avoiding the more traumatic real thing. Just outside the door, I stopped short in surprised delight. Then I forced myself to keep walking, as if the car waiting for me was one I saw every day, and not the kind of classic I normally admired from a safe financial distance.

It was a sparkling white convertible '56 T-Bird, revving its powerful engine in the sun. The top was down, the lanky guy driving it had a grin which made him look as if he was pretty sure he owned the world and all the women in it.

'Hey, pard, get your butt in here,' he called out.

I smiled and climbed into the car as if it was something I did every day, as if I had ever seen this good buddy of mine before.

'What'd you do, have a run-in with a combine this morning?' he asked, glancing over at my face. His voice had a distinct Texas drawl to it, and behind his aviator glasses, laughing, observant eyes watched me.

Was this a test? 'Nah,' I said, matching the casual tone, 'it's that new stuff Peg bought, that Burma Shave. It doesn't seem to have that same smooth lather as . . .' and my voice trailed off.

'Burma Shave, huh?'

'Yeah.'

He whistled a jingle as he navigated the little classic down gravel roads and through the climbing sunshine toward the base of the mountains. Then he turned the wheel of the T-Bird onto a drive with a sign which indicated we were entering Edwards Air Force Base at Muroc Lake. Aha, California, I thought.

'Well, you know what the Bird Dog always says,' said my driver.

And Bird Dog . . . bits and pieces of this morning's various confusing conversations popped back at me. Captain Birdell. Bill. The Captain will be here in ten minutes. Bill Birdell. Okay, I said to whoever was watching, I can put two and two together and come up with . . .

'No,' I said jokingly, 'what does the Bird Dog always say?'

'Whoo, Pard . . . lookit *that*!'

I followed his line of vision. Emerging from a low, one-story building was an eye-catching young woman. White short shorts skimmed the tops of her long, tanned legs. A bright blue, midriff hugging top made up the rest of the miniscule outfit, except for the high-heeled wedgies which kicked up little puffs of dust in the dry desert air as she strolled gracefully down the walk onto the road. Blonde hair in a page boy shone in the sunlight.

'Movin' in close to target, Pard, and I don't see no wedding ring,' said Bird Dog as he eased the T-Bird up alongside the girl.

'What good eyes you have, Grampa,' I remarked.

Bird Dog grinned at me, then turned his full attention to the girl, who was staring at the car, or him – definitely not me – with an expression of amused curiosity. And maybe something more.

Bird Dog idled the T-Bird and kept pace with her. 'Mornin', Sweet Pea,' he said genially.

'It's not Sweet Pea, it's Jeannie,' said the girl, hiding a smile.

'Well, then, howdy, pretty Jeannie. Like from a wishing bottle, huh? Like to make someone's wishes come true?'

Jeannie laughed and kept walking.

'My name is Captain Bill Birdell,' he persisted, 'but my friends call me Bird Dog.'

'What a surprise,' Jeannie remarked.

Bird Dog grinned at me again, then turned his attention to her. 'And this here facially wounded buddy of mine is Captain Tom Stratton.'

Jeannie glanced over at me and smiled.

'You've probably heard of us, Jeannie. Me and Tom here are the only two pilots in the entire U.S. Air Force brave enough to fly the X-2.'

We are? I thought.

'Is that so?' asked Jeannie, raising a carefully plucked eyebrow. 'What about Tony LaMott?'

'Aw, honey,' Bird Dog said sadly, 'please, *please* don't go breakin' my heart and tellin' me you've been led astray by that junior birdman.' He glanced at me as if for corroboration, so I nodded in agreement. 'Captain LaMott may wear a complicated lookin' wristwatch, but otherwise, he is not anywhere *near* close to bein' test pilot equipped. If you get my drift.'

Jeannie's laugh was clear and ringing in the morning quiet, and it seemed to give Bird Dog all the encouragement he needed to continue.

'Well, I don't know that I'd call it being led astray . . .' Her light eyes were flirtatious and innocent.

'Now, Jeannie of my dreams, this bein' Friday and all, and you knowin' Tony an' all, I haveta' assume that you're at the Ranch as his weekend guest, right?'

The ranch? I thought.

Jeannie gave Bird Dog one of those coy, up from under glances. 'Well . . .' she said, drawing the suspense out, 'I *am* staying at the Ranch.'

Bird Dog grinned. 'Then I'll expect to see you at the dance tonight, honey, and I'll expect you to save me a couple of the prime moves.'

A smile tugged at the corner of Jeannie's mouth.

Bird Dog saluted. 'The sonic booms you hear today will be dedicated to you, honey.' Then he put pedal to metal, and we screeched away.

Bird Dog kept an eye on Jeannie in the rear view mirror, but I was still thinking about what he had told her. I eyed him and tried to keep my voice from sounding nervous. 'Ah . . . don't you think that's laying it on a little thick?' I asked. 'I mean, the *only* two guys brave enough to fly the X-2?' Whatever *that* was, and I had the distinct feeling I really didn't want to know.

'Gotta impress the ladies, Pard, if you wanna score. Not that you care about that.' He winked at me. 'Besides, it's kinda true, anyway. LaMott hasn't broken the records we have.'

So . . . Tom was a flyboy. A record-breaking flyboy. A test pilot of some sort. And this was 1956, or thereabouts, so that meant Chuck Yeager time, guys like that. The sound barrier. Jesus, I thought, panic washing over me again. Whoever I was, I knew, just *knew* I didn't have that kind of right stuff. Right stuff . . . what was that, anyway?

'Uh, Bird Dog,' I said cautiously, 'ah . . . what if I told you I couldn't fly?'

'You sick?' He glanced quickly over at me.

'No,' I said shaking my head. 'Not . . . like that. I meant, what if I told you that when I woke up this morning I . . . I couldn't remember how to fly?'

Bird Dog squinted in thought for a moment. Then he flashed a grin in my direction. 'I like it, Pard. It's so jive crazy that it just might work.'

Work? I didn't know what he meant, but I felt relief begin to wash over me at his acceptance of what I'd said.

His next words took care of that. 'So who are we gonna pull it on?' he asked with a grin.

I realized he thought I was talking about a prank. Peg's words about practical jokes came back to me. This guy Tom Stratton must be some . . . joker, I thought, my heart sinking.

I gave it another try. 'It's not a joke,' I said.

Bird Dog threw back his head and laughed. 'Goddam,' he said, 'you really sound like you mean it.'

'I really do,' I said sincerely.

He looked over at me again and shook his head in admiration. 'Damn, Tom, that's exactly what makes you the best. That sincere look. That convincing tone.' He grinned again. 'If I could lie with a straight face like yours, my poontang rate would double.'

Bird Dog pulled the T-Bird to a halt in the middle of a dirt field. I sank down in my seat in despair, but he didn't seem to notice. He vaulted out of the car and stretched. 'Well, come on, buddy,' he said, 'let's get a move on it. There's birds and broads and a whole wide world waiting.'

What could I do? I got out of the T-Bird and fell into step with him. We reached the tarmac at the end of the field and began walking towards a group of men waiting at the other end. Suddenly, Bird Dog stopped dead in his tracks and stared at me. His look behind the glasses was intent, searching.

This is it, I thought, my heart in my mouth. I'm busted. I shouldn't have said anything, because now I'm going to have to explain, and I can't explain, because . . .

'Pard,' he said, that wide grin lighting up his face, 'you're a genius – this is the perfect one to pull on Weird Ernie!'

'Weird Ernie?' I echoed.

'Come on,' Bird Dog said, hurrying me along, 'this is gonna be good.'

CHAPTER THREE

We – that is me, and a whole group of flyers, fifties style – were sitting around inside an office in a one story building attached to a dome-like hangar. Not exactly luxurious, but the office had a nice view, great for looking at the field. And the planes. If you happened to like that sort of thing – me, my heart kept falling somewhere into the vicinity of my stomach.

The huge, gleaming silver beast outside had to be the B-50 Superfortress the guys were casually bantering about. Bird Dog had a handful of playing cards and was alternating between tricks he demonstrated and playing himself in some sort of strange kind of solitary poker. One of the other guys, the one called Tony, was concentrating on creating an elaborate cat's cradle with a couple of extra large rubber bands. Someone was talking about the ranch, and getting plastered later.

No one seemed particularly nervous or apprehensive. No one except me seemed to notice or mind that the thing outside was the size of the Empire State building, and didn't even look as if it could lift off the ground. Or that nestled beneath it like a baby gnat was another plane – this experimental rocket they all kept talking about. I couldn't be expected to fly these things, not a chance. That's what I told myself. Still, I couldn't tear my eyes away from them. I didn't know if it was fascination or terror. I just knew I was the only one in the room feeling it. But then, I was the imposter.

These flying cowboys were cut from the same cloth:

all thirty-ish, all tall and thin and lanky, their casual demeanors hiding an intense obsession with what they – we – were doing. And it definitely *was* we, because the face I had seen reflected in the mirror earlier, the face that had scared the living daylights out of me, was just like these faces; and everyone was talking to me as if I knew what I was talking about.

Another Captain, the one called Doug, said, 'How's Peg doing, Tom?'

No one replied.

'Hey, Earth to Tom . . .'

Me! 'Ah . . . what?' I looked up, startled.

'I said, how's Peg doing?'

'Oh, fine, fine,' I said hastily.

'Sally's getting a little nervous when I fly now. I figured it's 'cause she's expecting, too. How does Peg handle it?'

'Oh,' I said, scrambling for a suitable answer, 'like a trouper.'

'Well, I guess that's 'cause she's been through it before.'

Before? Oh, right, Mikey. 'Uh-huh.'

Doug grinned at me.

'And so've you. Man, are you casual about all this – I can't wait to see if ours is a boy or a girl!'

'Didn't you guys have an amnio?' The words popped out before I could think about what I was saying.

'A *what*?'

Right. This was 1956. No one here knew what an amniocentesis was: that was because it hadn't been invented yet.

Luckily for me, just at that moment, there was a distraction.

'Psst,' hissed one of the flyboys, 'they're coming.'

Bird Dog looked up from his hand of cards and winked at me. 'Ready, Pard?' he asked.

'Ready as I'll ever be,' I replied truthfully.

Bird Dog looked at me kind of strangely – I guessed it wasn't a very Tom kind of a reply.

Two men walked into the room. One was a heavyset, dark haired man with a moustache. He wasn't in uniform – instead, he wore a loud Hawaiian print shirt and sloppy blue trousers; everything overlapped on this man – his moustache, his belly, his eyebrows. He wore a puzzled frown. Dr Ernst. Weird Ernie. Who didn't look all that weird to me. Although I would learn that it was Ernst who was the man behind the X-2 project, and if going up in that little rocket wasn't weird, nothing was.

The man with him was just the opposite in appearance: neat to the point of pristine – wearing a white lab coat and a serious expression, his thinning hair neatly plastered back, everything in order. Dr Burger, I would find out. The flight surgeon.

'Good morning, men,' said Weird Ernie briskly. His garish clothes provided an odd contrast in a room full of men in monotone khaki flight suits and baseball caps. Except for one, Tony, who was suited up in a silver pressure suit.

Just then, I noticed the third man, a technician of some sort, I assumed, who had entered behind Weird Ernie and Dr Burger. He was an odd looking, impish sort of a man with dark unruly hair and a skewed grin. Under an ordinary white smock, he appeared to be wearing a black bow tie, the kind that goes with tuxedos more often than lab coats. No one paid any attention to him, however, and I was a little surprised when he seemed to single me out. He looked enquiringly at me, then gave a cheery little wave and a wink. I smiled back pleasantly.

Weird Ernie cleared his throat and consulted the clipboard he was carrying.

'Okay, men. We've been studying what happened last

29

time Captain Birdell went up. Dr Burger and I believe that the red fire-warning light that he saw when he reached Mach two-six was caused by inadequate insulation.'

There were a couple of good-natured boos from the flyboys.

'Told you to stop using that cheap stuff,' said the one called Tony, with a grin.

'What's the matter with you, Tony, don't you think tin foil is good enough material?' asked Doug.

Jesus, tin foil, how long had it been since I had heard anybody call it that?

'Anyway,' Dr Ernst continued as if there had been no interruption, 'we've re-wired the system, and we don't expect any further problems with it.'

There was some cat-calling and a bit of heckling laughter from the men in the room, and it struck me how supremely confident a person one had to be to do what they – we – were doing. I had no idea if I had that kind of confidence or not. For the first time, sitting in that room half-listening to the techno-language whizzing around me, I had a profound sense of loss of self: not only didn't I know my name or where or when I had come from, I didn't even know how I felt or thought or reacted to things. Tabula rasa – a very uncomfortable feeling.

Just then, I looked up and caught the strange technician in the bow tie looking at me in an intense, inquisitive manner. I fought down a feeling of panic: there was no way he could read my mind, there was no way he could see through my skull to the emptiness and doubts that lay inside. It must be coincidence.

'. . . so with the new wiring, as I said, we really don't anticipate any problems,' Weird Ernie repeated. I had no idea what I had missed in between the two identical statements – probably some convoluted description of the elements that went into the new wiring that would make it so much safer.

'Hey, Dr Ernst.' It was the silver suited Tony.

'Tony,' Weird Ernie acknowledged him.

Tony grinned, a cocky, self-confident grin. 'What's with all this "we" stuff, doc?' He glanced around the room and winked. 'You gonna be up there with me today?'

Weird Ernie smiled and shook his head. 'I wish I could be, Captain LaMott, I really do.' He paused. 'But as you all know . . .'

He lifted his hand and rapped his knuckles against his skull. I could hear a distinct metallic clank. '. . . my war wounds physically disqualify me from flying. Believe me, more than anyone else, I wish they didn't – I'd give my right arm to be up there.' He smiled again. 'Unfortunately, I already gave at the office.' And he rapped again.

There was a wave of laughter among the men.

'Now listen,' Dr Ernst continued, consulting his charts again, 'although we don't expect it to happen, if you *do* get a warning red light up around Mach two-six, I want you to shut down immediately, forget about the record. Just wait until the chase plane can catch up with you and look you over for any visible signs of fire.'

Bird Dog made a fancy motion with the cards, flipping them in a fan from hand to hand, just like a Vegas dealer. 'I don't know, Ernie,' he commented, 'a fella could get barbequed doing that.' He glanced over at Tony. 'Personally, you get a fire light, I'd recommend punching out, Tony. Else you might end up lookin' like one of the ranch's overdone T-bones!'

'You didn't punch out, Birdell,' Dr Ernst reminded him.

Bird Dog grinned that lazy grin. 'Yeah,' he drawled, 'but that's cause I'm a damn hero.'

The pilots laughed. Sometime during this bantering conversation, the odd technician in the bow tie had moved next to me. I jumped when he spoke: his approach had been utterly silent.

'I like this guy,' he said, gesturing in Bird Dog's direction. 'He reminds me of me in the old days.'

That seemed like a peculiar observation to me. There didn't appear to be the least resemblance between the laconic flyboy and this strange man, but what did I know? I shrugged agreeably and smiled.

'Okay, boys, let's get today's show on the road,' said Weird Ernie, and like a troop of obedient, overgrown boy scouts, we marched out into the hot, dry air. Follow the leader, I reminded myself. Do what they do. Fake it.

We clustered around a radio jeep under the huge wing of the B-50, gleaming in the morning sun, while Weird Ernie and Dr Burger climbed in.

'I guess this is it,' said Weird Ernie. 'If you men have no further questions . . .'

Bird Dog raised his hand. With a dead serious expression, he said, 'Ah, Dr Ernst, there *is* one thing I haven't mentioned before that I've been meaning to ask you about.'

'What's that, Birdell?' asked Weird Ernie.

'Ah, I know this is gonna sound a little weird . . .'

Weird Ernie – who may or may not have been aware of his nickname, and the hidden amusement value hearing the word weird gave to the pilots – looked a little leery all of a sudden.

'Yes?'

Bird Dog made a show of reluctance, then peered up at Weird Ernie with a serious expression. 'Okay, here goes. Is it possible that there's something, ah, I don't know what it could be, something at the edge of that Mach Three envelope that could be . . . affecting our minds?'

Weird Ernie still looked suspicious. 'Affecting your minds *how*?' he asked.

'Well,' said Bird Dog uncomfortably, 'it's like the faster I fly, the less I actually remember about it afterwards.'

Weird Ernie and Dr Burger exchanged puzzled looks.

Doug snapped his fingers. 'He's right, Doc,' he said. 'I've experienced that, too. And you know what? I'm starting to forget other things, too . . . like my wife's birthday. I never forgot Sally's birthday, not until I flew at Mach two-five!'

'That's so strange,' Tony LaMott chimed in, shaking his head as if he was utterly puzzled. 'I never really connected the two things before, but you know what? The last time I busted Mach two, I actually forgot where I parked my car!'

The other pilots nodded and murmured in agreement, and Weird Ernie and Dr Burger, after a puzzled look at each other, went into a huddled consultation.

'That's fascinating,' Weird Ernie said finally, 'fascinating. Dr Burger, could you design a test to quantify these apparent memory losses?'

Dr Burger nodded. 'I should be able to come up with something,' he said.

'Good,' Weird Ernie nodded decisively. 'This is an unexpected and most interesting development.' He surveyed the group of straight-faced pilots. 'Well, on with the day's work,' he said. 'And thank you, gentlemen.'

Weird Ernie threw the jeep into gear, and he and Dr Burger pulled away from the plane. As soon as the jeep was out of ear- and rear-view mirror shot, the pilots all looked at each other, and as one, erupted into howls of laughter.

'That was excellent, Bird Dog,' said Tony with admiration, 'and I do mean excellent!'

Bird Dog threw his arm around my shoulders. 'Well, y'all have Tom to thank for the idea,' he said.

Doug looked at me. 'But you didn't even say anything,' he said.

I shrugged modestly. 'I just gave the ball to Bird Dog and let him run with it,' I said. I punched my buddy lightly in the arm. 'He's better at bullshit than I am, anyway.'

'Since when?' hooted Doug.

Uh-oh, I thought, don't overdo it.

'Well, the best thing is, did you see Ernie's face?' Bird Dog laughed. 'Jesus, he swallowed it hook, line and slide rule!'

Still chuckling, Bird Dog turned and ducked underneath the open bomb bay. Then he disappeared up a ladder. I knew I was supposed to follow, and peered upwards into that cavernous unknown, wondering if I was afraid of heights or afraid of flying. Wondering just what the hell I was supposed to do, now that joke time was over and everyone was getting down to the real business at hand.

I felt rather than saw someone beside me, and when I turned to look, it was the technician with the tuxedo bow tie. I jumped. I hadn't seen him in the jeep with Weird Ernie, but I hadn't seen him stay on the field with the pilots, either. The man seemed to have the ability to move around like a cat, silent and unseen.

He peered up into the bomb bay, then looked back over at me, and I could see his eyes bright with some kind of glee. 'Isn't this a kick in the butt?' he said.

'I guess that's one description,' I replied. Suddenly, I

34

wanted to get away from his too-inquisitive stare. I did my best with a casual smile and shrug, then I started up the ladder, following Bird Dog into whatever lay in store for me up there.

CHAPTER FOUR

Climbing up into the big belly of the B-50 Superfortress *was*, as the odd little technician had said, a kick in the butt. It was all so *unreal* – it made me feel as if I was walking into an old movie, a war movie, or maybe just any young boy's fantasy. But despite the thrill of it, it was also utterly terrifying, because nothing, absolutely nothing about it was in the least familiar to me. The cavernous interior looked severely under-equipped to my inexperienced eyes; and when I made my way forward into the cockpit, the instrument panels in front of the two pilot's seats appeared primitive compared to . . . compared to *what*? Once again, I came to a frustrating, screeching halt at the impenetrable wall of my own memory. I simply didn't *know*.

'Well, come on, Pard, what are you waiting for?' Bird Dog, looking casual and perfectly at home in the pilot's seat, motioned me in next to him.

'Nothing,' I said, and slid obediently into the co-pilot's seat.

Of course, I didn't have the faintest idea what came next, or what I was supposed to do, so I just watched Bird Dog out of the corner of my eye and mimicked his motions. Like Bird Dog, I strapped myself into a harness-like safety contraption, then tugged on a nose-cone gas mask that hung around my neck. Then I waited.

'All set back there?' Bird Dog called out. A couple of affirmative answers came from the technicians in the bay. 'Okay, let's do it.'

36

I waited and prayed, and to my surprise, my prayer was – at least temporarily – answered. It seemed to be all Bird Dog's show. Using the archaic-looking yoke in front of him, and a rather simple set of levers and switches, Bird Dog taxied the Superfortress along the runway. Then, with a minimum of effort – or so it seemed to me – he took the bulky plane easily up into the air. All I had to do, apparently, was sit back in the co-pilot's seat. I relaxed enough to take a good look through the broad glass nose of the plane. The view as we rose was breathtaking; the horizon seemed to expand, then turn pale, then just drop away below us. Puffs of white clouds got thinner and thinner, then disappeared altogether as we climbed higher.

Tony LaMott came up from the back and crouched between our two seats.

'How's it hanging, you two?' he asked genially. 'We about ready to blast off?'

'Just about,' Bird Dog agreed.

'Good,' Tony grinned, ''cause I'm itching to get a crack at that record of yours.'

'Take it easy, junior,' said Bird Dog. 'By the way, Captain, I've been meaning to ask you, when'd you go into the import business?'

Tony seemed puzzled. 'What are you talking about?' he asked.

Bird Dog smiled a sly little smile. 'Oh, come on, Tony, this is me, the Bird Dog! You know you can't keep secrets like that from me – I'm talkin' about that long-legged blonde honey you got stayin' at the ranch this weekend.'

Tony just shook his head in good natured disbelief. 'Jesus, Tom,' he said to me, 'what does he do, smell them coming?'

I shrugged.

'It's a gift, son, a blessed natural gift,' Bird Dog said.

'Kinda' like, well, like a bird dog flushing a quail.' He winked at Tony. 'You might acquire that gift yourself, some day, if you work real hard.'

Tony just shook his head again. 'Unbelievable,' he said. He peered at the simple round gauges on the pilots' panels. 'Looks like it's about that time, kids, I gotta mount up.'

'That's one way of puttin' it,' grinned Bird Dog as Tony disappeared through the narrow passage that led to the bomb bay.

I glanced over my shoulder a minute later and saw a couple of the white-coated lab technicians helping Tony into the tiny cockpit of the X-2, and restrained a shudder. The thing looked no bigger than a toy, and just about as solid. I couldn't restrain that shudder any longer when I saw them lock the fiberglass bubble into place and give Tony the thumbs up. It made me grateful that whatever it was that was happening to me, I seemed to have a guardian spirit watching over me. After all, that could have been me climbing into that X-2, not Tony.

Come to think of it, I told myself reflectively, this really might not be so bad after all. I wasn't in the X-2. I wasn't in the chase plane, which Doug Walker of the pregnant wife was flying. I wasn't – thank God – in the pilot's seat of the B-50. That was Bird Dog's job. All I had to do, it seemed, was sit here and enjoy the scenery and the excitement of it all. Not bad, I told myself again, actually beginning to get into the flow of things – here I am, surrounded by some of the most exciting action known to man, one in an elite group of test pilots on the threshold of making aviation history . . . and I don't even have to fly!

Bird Dog lifted his hands off the yoke and stretched. Then he began to unbuckle his harness. I wondered if I should do the same.

Bird Dog got up out of his seat and turned towards the bay. He glanced over his shoulder and saw me staring at him. 'She's all yours, Pard,' he said.

'*What*?' So much for relaxing. I fought to keep the panic out of my voice.

'Take her on up to twenty-five,' Bird Dog told me casually. 'Mother Nature's callin' me, and I gotta answer.' Without waiting for a reply, he disappeared, leaving me alone in the cockpit. Suddenly nothing seemed fun or easy, and I reversed my opinion that there was any kind of guardian spirit looking after old . . . *whoever* the hell I really was.

I looked down at the primitive yoke in front of me. I put my hands tentatively on it, and it began to wobble unsteadily back and forth. I snatched my hands back. Oh, God, I thought, if you're there, *please* make a minute for me. I waited, but nothing happened. The yoke went from a slow wobble to a faster vibrating motion, echoing the increase in my heart beat. I watched it with growing horror – what was I supposed to do?

The B-50 had to be on some sort of automatic pilot, I thought, didn't it? Did they even have auto-pilot then? I had no idea, and I sat there, frozen, as the big plane continued its climb. I felt helpless, paralyzed. Now I was even frightened to grab the yoke again, terrified that if I did, I would send us plummeting to earth. I could feel the sweat beading on my forehead, and even the oxygen nose cone didn't seem to make my breathing any less shallow and rapid.

I could see Doug Walker's F-86 chaser trailing out to the side of the Superfortress, and wondered if he could see into the B-50, if he could read the panic on my face. Then, suddenly, I felt the right wing of the big plane begin to drop, and we began to curve, off to the right.

'Mother Hen,' I heard Doug's voice come over the

radio in the cockpit. 'Mother Hen, Chase One. Is there a change in the flight profile? Over.'

The B-50 continued to turn, and I knew I had to do something. I finally forced myself to grab the yoke and hold on; the intense pressure made it extremely difficult to do that, and I made no effort to try to figure out how to answer Doug.

His voice crackled over the radio again. 'Bird Dog, you reading me?'

Doug's voice faded, and I was glad – it was one less thing for me to think about. But Weird Ernie's cut in immediately. 'Mother Hen. Edwards,' said Ernie. 'Radar indicates you are in a forty degree per minute turn to the right. Are you experiencing a problem?'

Oh, boy, if you only knew, I thought. The plane seemed set on a course of its own, and it obviously was the wrong course. Okay, I thought, be logical. If I was making an unscheduled right, the logical thing to do was correct it . . .

I held my breath and turned the yoke to the left. For a moment, nothing happened at all. Then suddenly, the big Superfortress responded, and the right wing began to lift . . . and lift . . . and lift . . .

'Ooooooh . . . Jesus!' I gasped. I could feel that we were going up too fast, it was all wrong; I was dizzy, out of breath. My heart accelerated into the danger zone, and sweat poured down my face.

I could hear the surprised yells of the men in the back of the bay, as they went tumbling from one side of the plane to the other, thrown completely off balance by the plane's steep climb and abrupt turn. This was like some kind of rollercoaster ride, but it was a hell of a lot more frightening, because there was literally no one in control. *I* certainly didn't know how to put on the brakes, and bring us to a safe, gentle stop.

'Bird Dog!' I could hear that Doug's voice had a worried edge to it as it came over the radio again into the cockpit. 'Bird Dog! Tom! What's going on? Can you read me? Over!'

I yanked the control yoke desperately back towards the right again, in an attempt to correct what I had done. Once again, there was that heart stopping, breathless pause before anything at all happened. Then I could feel the left wing began to lift, and just when it seemed that the plane was going to level out, I realized I had pulled the yoke too far again. The left wing continued its ascent until the Superfortress began a steep, banking turn to the right. I could hear the men in back trying to protect themselves from being bounced off the walls again.

Just at that moment, bracing himself with both hands, Bird Dog managed to climb back into the cockpit. He threw himself into his seat and hurriedly fastened his protective harness.

'What the hell is the matter, Tom?'

'I can't fly!' I yelled.

Bird Dog didn't bother to reply. He simply grabbed the yoke and wrestled with it. I don't know what he did, but within a few moments, I could feel the plane level out, its big nose headed straight on. The Superfortress was back on course, climbing in a steady normal fashion. Bird Dog put his head set back on and looked over at me.

'What'd you say?' he asked me. 'What happened?'

I took a deep breath. Telling him the truth seemed to be my only hope, and perhaps his as well. 'I told you this morning that I forgot how to fly,' I said grimly. I couldn't go on faking this, not when there were people's lives at stake. Not even if my confession landed me in the rubber room, not even if by some miracle this really did turn out to be a dream.

Before Bird Dog could reply, Weird Ernie's voice came screeching over the radio. 'Mother Hen. Edwards. Do you have a problem? Over!' He sounded almost as worried as I felt.

Bird Dog frowned and studied my face carefully for a moment. He must have seen the drained, post-panic expression, and for just a second, I could see a flicker of doubt cross his mind. Then he grinned, that normal cocky grin of his.

'Christ almighty,' he said, 'you dumb son of a bitch, you actually had me goin' for about a second there! You know what, you're crazier than Weird Ernie, Pard, and that's goin' some!'

'Mother Hen!'

Bird Dog keyed his mike and winked at me. 'Edwards. Mother Hen. We must've had a bubble in the hydraulic system back there – for a little bit, this bird was flyin' more like a mack truck. Whatever it was, she burped it out. On course, we're continuing our climb to twenty-five thousand. Over.'

'Glad to hear it, Mother Hen.'

Bird Dog clicked off his mike and looked over at me. 'Hey, Pard?'

I braced myself for him to ask me about what I had said. I was trying to figure out how I could tell him what was happening without sounding like a raving lunatic, when Bird Dog said conspiratorially, 'It was a real nice try. But you just save it for Weird Ernie, 'cause it's never gonna really work on me.'

I realized with a sinking feeling that he would never, never believe me. Tom was a joker, and it was all too . . . crazy. That was the only word. Well, I thought, as long as he stayed at the controls, it would be okay. 'No?' I said.

'Tom,' he said, shaking his head in reproach, 'how long

42

we been buddies? You oughta know by now that my mama didn't raise her little boy to be a fool.' Then he laughed, and turned his attention back to the controls.

So much for honesty, I thought. But I felt compelled to say, 'Just don't ask me to fly.'

Bird Dog snorted in derision. 'Right,' he said.

I relaxed a little, and concentrated on getting my heart rate back down to a mere double-time. A few minutes later, as the clock ticked down to 9:30, Bird Dog switched on the mike. 'Edwards. Mother Hen. Level at twenty-five thousand.'

'Roger, Mother Hen.' Weird Ernie's voice, carrying up from the dry lake bed so far below, sounded slightly distorted. 'You're clear to drop.'

Then a very faint pinging sound came over the radio, and Bird Dog laughed. 'He's rappin' his head for luck again,' he said.

'I hope it works,' I said.

Bird Dog threw me a peculiar look. 'Why wouldn't it work, Pard? It has every time before.' Then he spoke into the mike again. 'Tony, my old buddy, how you doin' back there?'

'Just fine, Captain.'

'Good,' said Bird Dog, ''cause I'm gettin' tired of haulin' your butt around.'

'I'm ready any time you are, Captain,' Tony said.

Bird Dog grinned at me and said to Tony, 'Well then, I'm just gonna cut you loose, and we'll see which one of us gets to that little leggy blonde number you got stashed back at the ranch first.'

'Hey, Captain?' Tony said.

'Yeah?'

'Turn around. I've got something I think you should see.'

Bird Dog and I both turned and looked back into the

43

bomb bay to see what Tony was talking about. From inside the fiberglass cockpit of the little X-2, I could see that Tony was holding up a gloved middle finger in a timeless salute.

Bird Dog grinned and spoke into the mike. 'I'll take that to mean a "roger" for the drop, LaMott.'

Tony grinned back, and I saw him give the thumbs up signal. Then I noticed something else that puzzled me. For protection from the suction the X-2's drop would inevitably cause, all the technicians were now strapped into the canvas seats that lined the fuselage. All except one.

Beyond them all, standing far back in the bomb bay, I could see the oddly observant technician just standing, not secured to anything. His position was precarious, to say the least. He stood directly behind the X-2's tail, where he would be certain to have a perfect view of the drop. Perfect, and perfectly dangerous.

He saw me looking at him, and he gave a little grin and a wave. Just then the slipstream whipped his white smock open. He was actually wearing a tuxedo underneath. Who the hell *was* this guy?

I waved back, then turned to Bird Dog. 'Ah . . . is everyone back there okay where they're at?' I asked.

Bird Dog glanced towards the back for an instant. 'Looks fine to me,' he said. Then he faced the controls again. 'Two forty indicated. Here we go, ladies.' He paused, then began his countdown.

'Drop in ten . . . nine . . . eight . . .'

I turned towards the back again, and saw Tony making a last minute adjustment in his safety harness. He didn't look at all nervous.

'. . . seven . . . six . . . five . . .'

Better him than me, I thought.

'. . . four . . . three . . . two . . .'

The desert sky was brilliant blue, clear, stretching endlessly out in front of us. The last frontier, I thought. The phrase rang a faint bell in my head, but I couldn't remember where I had heard it before.

'. . . one. Bombs away!'

The X-2 dropped suddenly from the Superfortress. For a moment, I couldn't see anything at all, and then Tony, now clear of the B-50, fired off two rockets. The X-2 shot by us in a flashing streak, and both the B-50 and the B-86 chaser plane made us look as though we were standing still. The X-2 roared, leaving a stream of flame and white smoke in its wake.

Bird Dog and I watched as the experimental rocket veered and climbed towards the heavens, breaking the sound barrier with a deafening boom, and disappearing into a pinpoint of light.

Bird Dog kept looking till there was nothing left to see. Then he said reverently, 'Ride her, cowboy.'

It sounded like a prayer.

CHAPTER FIVE

There was nothing but wide, empty blue sky all around us, and at the moment, things were quiet inside the big Superfortress. It may have been the satisfaction of Tony's successful drop and take-off, or it may have just been an audio contrast to the resounding sonic boom he had created when he broke the sound barrier and disappeared. At any rate, it seemed to me as if there had been a collective sigh of relief after the X-2 had dropped from the belly. Now, there was silence.

I decided to take advantage of this in-between moment, to get myself away from the controls I didn't know how to use, and see if I could regroup a little and figure out just what the hell I was going to do next.

I unbuckled the canvas harness straps and pulled them off my shoulders. Then I got up and stretched, rotating my shoulders around a few times, trying to get my tense muscles to relax a little. It was definitely uphill work. 'My turn for the head,' I said to Bird Dog, and pointed towards the bay.

'Don't get lost,' he replied seriously. 'Wouldn't want you droppin' outta that bay without a plane or a chute, now.'

'Huh?' I stared at him startled. 'What are you talking about?'

'Well, Pard,' Bird Dog said, that laconic drawl laced with mischief, 'all I meant was, what with your sudden and *intense* loss of memory and everything . . .' he winked at me as though we were sharing some terrifically funny inside joke, 'I just figured I might havta' remind you where the head *was*.'

'Oh,' I said, relieved. He was kidding. Or at least, he *thought* he was kidding. 'I get it now.' It was more ironic than funny, but who was I to burst his bubble? 'Very funny.'

'You know me, Pard, I always am,' Bird Dog said with that easy self confidence which marked his approach to . . . well, in the short time I'd known him, seemingly everything in life, from life-endangering experimental flight to blonde women who had arrived at the base with someone else in mind.

I nodded in agreement. 'Right back,' I said, and turned to climb through the narrow confines of the passageway that led from the cockpit to the cavernous bomb bay.

The various technicians working there greeted me with casual familiarity, throwing comments about the current flight in my direction. It was a little bit like playing ping-pong blindfolded or juggling seven objects with one hand tied behind my back – trying to field their questions and provide answers without really answering; trying to act like I knew what they were talking about, and trying to keep anyone from noticing that I didn't know their names, or what they did, or if we were friends or merely nodding acquaintances.

'Clean exit, huh, Captain?' said one of the technicians, a balding, cheerful man.

'Very clean,' I agreed.

'Think Captain La Mott is gonna break the record?' This came from a wiry little tech with a pocketful of pens clipped on a plastic holder.

'Good question,' I replied seriously. 'I just don't know.' I paused. 'What do you think?' Somewhere I must have learned that answering a question with a question

47

was a good way to distract someone from the fact that you didn't have an answer.

The technicians looked – as one – judicious. Maybe they weren't used to the flyboys asking their opinions. One of them finally said, 'I kind of think this might be the flight.'

'Me, too,' I agreed. Hell, why not agree? They certainly knew more about this process than *I* did. I looked at the men in the group and suddenly I realized that the peculiar technician wearing the tuxedo wasn't anywhere to be seen.

'Hey,' I said, 'where's the . . .' then I stopped. If I should know who *they* were, then I should know who he was, too; I couldn't very well ask 'where's the weirdo with the tuxedo?' without arousing some suspicions. Besides, if he had dropped from his precarious position out of the bomb bay along with the X-2, I was sure someone would have noticed it by now.

'Where's the what, Captain?'

'Oh, nothing,' I said hastily.

Just then, I spotted the door to the head and escaped gratefully inside. It was just like any bathroom on any commercial flight, less luxurious, naturally, but with that same feeling of totally cramped, claustrophobic space, and that same hideous ambience – the one that makes you think that when you flush, you may just disappear along with the waste products.

I rinsed my hands and face, and grabbed a scratchy brown paper towel to dry myself off. Then I looked in the dingy little mirror and saw . . . Tom Stratton. Square of jaw, dark of hair, lanky of frame; and possessing, just now, a very worried look in his probably normally steely eyes – really my expression in his eyes, I supposed. It was the eeriest feeling, and I had the sudden realization that *this* was the real reason I had to find out who I was,

48

where I was from, and get the hell back there. Because looking at that reflection, I just knew that if I had to wake up for too many more days and see someone else's face in the mirror, I would definitely crack . . .

Okay, I told Tom's reflection, don't worry. Whoever you are, you'll get yourself back, I swear. And I'll get myself back. And then everyone will be happy. You and me, we'll be happy. Peg and Mikey and the unborn baby. And all the flyboys, who would be infinitely less endangered than they unwittingly were at the moment – they'll be happy, too. But despite the promise, the eyes I saw reflected back at me still looked worried. Well, I thought, too bad – I couldn't very well stay hidden in the head for the rest of the flight.

I opened the door and promptly came face to face with the missing, enigmatic technician. He was lounging casually against the metal beamed side of the bomb bay, examining his fingernails.

'Howdy,' I said. It seemed like something Tom would say.

The technician stared quizzically at me. 'Howdy yourself,' he finally replied. 'So. How's it going up there in the cockpit?'

For some reason, the question – or maybe it was the way it was said – made me uneasy. 'Ah . . . just fine.'

'Really?' His dark button eyes seemed to bore right into mine, and my nervousness grew.

'Oh,' I shrugged and grinned, giving a pallid imitation of Bird Dog's devil-may-care attitude, 'well, me and Bird Dog, we may do some screwin' around up there, but you know how it is . . .'

'Not exactly,' he said, a peculiarly serious expression crossing his face.

This isn't working. 'Hey,' I said, attempting to lighten the tone and switch the direction of this conversation with some diversionary tactics, 'what's the deal with the fancy dress? How come you're wearing a tux under your lab coat?'

His serious expression grew even more somber. 'Don't you know?' he asked.

I scrambled desperately for some sort of logical explanation or reply. Had there been a big dance or something the night before? How would I know? I was brand new to this place. I had only arrived about four hours before. But no, that couldn't be it – no one else was decked out or fatigued looking; no one had mentioned it. No. I shook my head.

The technician seemed suddenly as unnerved as I was, surveying me as if I was something that had just landed from another planet. Then he abruptly switched gears again. He grinned crookedly and shrugged his shoulders. 'Just one of life's little mysteries, huh, *Captain*?' I noticed that he peered very intensely at me as he said this.

I smiled back at him uneasily. 'I guess so,' I replied.

'Hmmm,' he said.

'Well, I'd better be getting back to work,' I said, easing myself back, eager to get myself away from his prying eyes and doubting attitude. Or was I just imagining these things? I didn't know, and I certainly didn't trust myself to be the very best judge of reality at the moment. 'See you later,' I said casually, then restrained myself from racing back to pitfalls that surely awaited me in the cockpit.

Of course, Bird Dog seemed perfectly at ease and perfectly in control. I slipped back into my seat and reharnessed the canvas straps, trying to act like I knew precisely what I was doing.

Bird Dog glanced over and nodded. 'Perfect timing, Pard,' he remarked.

For what? I thought.

Just then, Tony's voice came over the radio. 'Fifty thousand,' he said, 'Mach on-three and accelerating. Nosing over.'

Bird Dog made a gesture of easing the stick forward. 'Go, Tony,' he said quietly. He looked over at me again, then pointed through the cockpit window, up into the heavens. I nodded.

Tony's voice crackled over the airwaves again. 'One-eight. One-nine.' He paused. Despite the machismo requirements of the job, I could hear that a note of excitement had entered his voice as he said, 'Mach-two.' And paused again.

'Take it gentle,' said Bird Dog to no one in particular.

'She's leveling off,' Tony's disembodied voice announced. 'Sixty-five thousand. Sixty-six . . .'

'Uh-huh,' said Bird Dog, nodding with satisfaction.

'Level at seventy-one thousand,' Tony announced. 'Mach two point four. On profile.'

'Time to . . .' said Bird Dog.

'. . . start my run,' said Tony.

'Third rocket time,' Bird Dog said excitedly. 'And away we go . . .'

'Mach two-five . . . two-six . . .'

I could feel the excitement building, not just in Tony's voice, but in the cockpit where Bird Dog and I sat listening.

'No fire light,' Tony announced with satisfaction. 'Looks like we beat that gremlin . . .'

'All right!' I said, getting into the spirit of the occasion.

'Mach two-seven. Skin temperature is at . . .' Tony paused, 'eight hundred.' He paused again, then his voice came back over the air, sounding a little puzzled. 'I think I smell something . . .'

'Huh?' Bird Dog's brow furrowed.

A buzzing sounded. 'Fire warning light!' Tony's voice was tense, but not panicked.

'Turn the rockets . . .' Bird Dog began.

'Rockets . . . off.' There was a breathless pause, then his voice returned, relieved. 'Everything looks a-okay now. Mach two-four. Two-three.'

I glanced over at Bird Dog, who seemed immensely relieved.

'I think it was another false alarm,' Tony said. 'Where are you, Dougie?'

This question was directed to Doug Walker, trailing Tony in the chaser plane.

'Five miles behind you,' Doug's voice announced, 'at thirty thousand.'

'Roger,' Tony replied. 'Coming back to you for a look see.'

'No!' Bird Dog shouted immediately, 'Tony, don't turn below Mach-two!' He pounded on the yoke and said, 'Oh, Jesus! Tony!'

I had no idea what was going on, but there was no mistaking the panic in Bird Dog's voice.

Then we heard Tony's voice, distorted and breaking up, barely filtering through the mike. 'Oh . . . I . . . lost her!'

'Eject!' Bird Dog screamed. 'Tony, eject!'

'Oh, Christ,' I gasped, as the out-of-control X-2 hurtled past us, plummeting towards earth. It became a spinning white dot which disappeared down as rapidly as it had up, when it had made its climb towards the heavens.

I could hear Doug shouting from the mike in the chaser plane, 'Punch out, Tony, punch out!'

From the back of the B-50, we could hear the technicians shouting, as if anything anyone said or did now could be of use to Tony LaMott. We could all only pray now that he had chosen to eject, not go down in flames; and that he had ejected in time.

'Let's go,' Bird Dog sounded grim.

I just nodded.

Bird Dog worked the levers and yoke in grim silence, and as we headed back to the base, and the earth came finally into view again, we could see a billowing cloud of black smoke rising from the dry lake bed.

'Oh, Jesus . . .' I whispered.

Then we could begin to make out a convoy – the jeeps of Weird Ernie and Dr Burger, and an ambulance crew as they raced towards the scene of the crash.

'Holy Christ,' I said softly.

'You can say that again!' Bird Dog agreed, his voice suddenly excited, 'Along with an amen! Take a look at what I see, Pard!'

And following the direction of Bird Dog's glance, suddenly I could see it too: half a mile beyond the smoking wreck, there it was, white and beautiful, sil-houetted against the blue sky. Tony LaMott's parachute drifted slowly, safely down to earth.

I could feel myself start to breathe again, could hear the whoops of triumph from the technicians in the bomb bay as they, too, spotted Tony descending.

Bird Dog pounded happily on the yoke and switched on the mike. 'Mother Hen to Chaser, do you see what I see?'

Doug Walker's voice floated back to us, clear and ringing. 'Chaser to Mother Hen, I sure as shit do!' And he let out a rebel yell which Bird Dog echoed. So did I.

For guys whom I had never set eyes on until a couple of hours before, I felt awfully bonded, I realized. I still had no idea why I was here, but even though I wanted desperately to get my own self and life back, the relief I felt was overwhelming. I had the sudden feeling that

53

there was something pretty terrific about being here at this time in history, witnessing what I had just witnessed.

'Well, Pard,' Bird Dog relaxed and smiled, 'I guess we got through another week.'

I smiled back and gave the requisite thumbs up sign.

'So next week,' Bird Dog continued, 'it's your turn again.'

I felt a wave of panic breaking over me. 'Ah . . .'

He looked cheerful and determined. 'And I just know that you're gonna break that record. Aren't you?'

I grinned weakly and, reversing my previous thoughts about being here now, prayed devoutly that somehow, I would be home – wherever that was – for the weekend.

CHAPTER SIX

Looking back on things later that evening, I reflected to myself that it was pretty amazing that I had actually made it through my first day as Tom Stratton as successfully as I had. A life's road lined with trip-ups, pitfalls, potential disasters and death had stretched blankly in front of me from the minute of awakening; and somehow, on instinct and auto-pilot – no pun intended – and maybe just some fluky dumb luck, I had maneuvered through the mine field without getting caught. Maybe I could breathe a temporary sigh of relief, and congratulate myself.

Not that any of that meant I could stop, for one second, trying to figure out what had happened or how to discover and rectify the situation; I had obviously no intention of remaining in the here and now – or there and then – one moment longer than absolutely necessary. Still, at least for the evening, I could relax a little and enjoy what appeared to be the regular Friday night routine for the pilots at Edwards.

And from listening to the guys discuss their casually thrown together plans, what *that* seemed to mean was an evening together – some fun time out with the wives and girl friends, some serious drinking, some dancing, some hearty food of the pre-cholesterol conscious kind, and more talk – naturally – about flying. That part of it I would do my best to avoid.

We, Peg and me, that is, had left Mikey in the care of a sulky pubescent babysitter (Peg 'reminded' me that her parents, whom we apparently knew only slightly, were currently having a small volcanic eruption in their marriage caused by his attention to a certain sultry brunette who worked at the PX, and that Judy, the babysitter, was having a hard time dealing with it) and headed out for the evening.

We waved goodbye, and then I ushered Peg into Tom's turquoise and white Chevy and headed for a good time. More specifically, for the 'Ranch,' that same low slung bar and grill where Bird Dog had honed in on the visiting blonde Jeannie earlier this morning. It was a long, smoke-filled combination restaurant and bar, filled with fliers and their wives and girls. All, no doubt, grateful to be greeting Friday night still breathing. Fifties standards and country western music poured from the jukebox, and there was a general air of tension being released, kind of like air escaping from a balloon.

This was obviously the place to be, and everyone from the base seemed to know it. Even Weird Ernie and the flight surgeon, Dr Burger, could be spotted, deep in serious and no-doubt technical conversation beside the Western type bar. With its back wall, which featured a wall full of calf-roping and barrel-riding pictures, some silver buckles and trophies, and mounted lariats and spurs, it hardly seemed like the right atmosphere for scientific talk, but then, what did I know?

Peg and I were seated at a rough wood table in the corner, along with Bird Dog, Doug Walker and his wife Sally. We were in the process of polishing off huge platters of juicy steaks, and the accompanying thick-cut French fries and greasy onion rings. Not a green vegetable in sight, unless you counted the tiny, un-touched bowls of warmed up canned peas that came along with each dinner plate, and remained conspicuously ignored.

Bird Dog stretched his lanky legs out to their full length, and tipped his chair back at a dangerous angle, turning a sharp surveying eye to the dance floor. 'Maybe the X-2 didn't get that boy today, but I can tell you something – *she's* sure gonna be able to auger him in.' He drained a long-neck bottle of beer and gestured towards the dance floor.

I followed his line of vision and saw Tony LaMott, obviously recovered from his earlier experience. In a civilian shirt and khakis he was dancing, well, it was actually more like standing in place and hugging, with the blonde named Jeannie.

'Think he's talking about his near-brush with death?' Doug said snidely.

'There's nothing quite so impressive,' Sally winked.

'Or sexy,' Peg nodded.

'Right, till you live through it,' Sally said.

'Hog tied and down,' Bird Dog said, shaking his head in disgust.

'Think so?' Peg asked.

'Well, come on now, look at him for yourself, he's got that pitiful sick calf look!' Bird Dog waved an arm to flag a passing waitress. He motioned to the beer bottles. ''Nother round, sweetheart,' he said.

I let him go ahead and order, so it wouldn't seem obvious. But I had no intention of drinking much at all – talk about a sure fire way to slip up!

Sally, not quite as obviously pregnant as Peg, but still happily showing, was snuggled into the curve of Doug's arm, watching the action all around. She looked mischievously from the dance floor to Bird Dog, then at us. 'Here we go, gang, I can always tell – the Bird Dog's about to pounce. Again!'

'Well, shoot,' Bird Dog said in good-natured defense of himself, 'I gotta keep an eye on things, you know!

Besides, Tony's the only pilot left in the B.O.Q. Be awful lonesome there without him.'

Peg giggled. 'Come on, Bird Dog, how on earth would you know? From what I hear, you never sleep in the B.O.Q. yourself!'

Bird Dog flashed her a mock reproving look, then turned his attention to me. 'Hey, Pard, what kinda vicious rumors you been spreadin' about me?'

'Just the truth,' I assured him.

Bird Dog snorted. He took a long swallow from the full bottle the waitress had plonked down in front of him, then got up. 'Well, folks,' he tipped his cowboy hat in the general direction of the table, 'I got work to do.'

'Some work,' Doug laughed.

We all watched as Bird Dog sort of dance-walked across that sawdust covered wooden floor, snaking between the couples there. With his cowboy boots adding another inch to his height, and a natural swagger, he cut a kind of mythical movie Western figure as he went. I watched with amusement as he tapped Tony lightly on the shoulder, and whirled Jeannie away in a Texas two-step. Tony looked in our direction and shrugged good naturedly. Then he moved towards the bar.

'Our turn, sweetheart,' Doug said, and helped Sally to her feet. They moved out onto the dance floor too, and Peg and I were left alone at the table.

Peg reached over and put her hand on mine. It was a perfectly natural gesture, an affectionate, spontaneous touch between two supposedly intimate people, but it caught me off guard. It brought me back to another reality of this situation, the reality of the marriage in which I was masquerading. I smiled, but I covertly studied the woman beside me, the woman who was Tom's wife.

Peg had a slightly wistful smile on her face as she

58

watched her friends on the dance floor, swaying to the music. She glanced briefly at me, her eyes shining, then looked back towards the floor. It was obvious in every look, in every move and touch, that Peg was deeply in love with ... Tom. Her husband. And that had to be really hard on her, even without harboring a suspicion that the man she had woken up with wasn't really that husband.

From what I had been through in just this one day, from that brief exchange between Peg and Sally, I knew that every time he walked out that door in the morning, she had to wonder if she would ever see him again. Every time there was a sonic boom or a black cloud or a trail of white smoke in the sky above the lake bed, every time there was the sound of a siren, she – and the other wives – must have felt their hearts in their throats, waiting to see who crashed, waiting to see what the outcome was. Waiting to see if one of them had been made a widow.

From what I had seen so far, Peg seemed to be a naturally upbeat, cheerful woman, and I wondered how she managed to hide her fear so well. I supposed it was just a part of the job of being married to a test pilot, but it certainly couldn't be the easiest part. I watched her watching the dancers and realized with a little shock, she's beautiful, too. And she was. A soft blonde with an infinitely sweet face, that kind of open, innocent face that went with the times. Or the movies of the times, anyway. She had her shiny blonde hair done in curly bangs, the rest swept back in a modified pony tail, curled too. Her maternity dress was a soft blue, much like her eyes, with a sweet lace collar framing her collar bone. Peaches and cream complexion, almost no make-up except a faint glimmer of pink on her generous mouth.

I suddenly had the impulse to tell her how beautiful she was, but I knew she would never believe me. No pregnant woman ever does – all they see are the stretch marks and the fatigue on their faces. Somehow I knew that it was something you had to keep reminding them of, but that the words were never quite enough to convince them.

'Would you like to dance?' I asked impulsively.

Peg turned her face towards me, with an expression of surprise. '*What?*'

I motioned towards the floor, then back at her. 'You know,' I said, 'dance.'

Peg pointed to her own abdomen. 'With this stomach?' she said. 'You've got to be joking, Tom.'

I shrugged. 'I can reach around it,' I told her.

'Seriously?' Her face lit up with a delighted smile. 'Okay,' she said, and gave me her hand to be helped up from the table.

We moved out onto the dance floor together and began a smooth, slow slide to the strains of the 'Moonglow' theme from 'Picnic'.

Peg seemed quietly delighted as we swayed together, and I wondered if Tom never took her dancing, or what. It wasn't so hard to reach around her, and she felt good in my arms. She nestled her head comfortably on my shoulder and sighed. We danced well together, moving smoothly and gracefully around the floor. It was all very sweet, very innocent, very romantic. I knew it should make me very uncomfortable, but my pleasure at her nearness outweighed the mitigating circumstances.

Suddenly, Peg stopped and pulled back. She looked up at me with a look both happy and puzzled. 'Okay, Mister,' she said, 'I want to know just who you've been dancing with.'

'What?' I replied, startled. 'What do you mean?'

Peg looked at me reprovingly. 'Oh, come on, Tom. You may be the best test pilot in the entire Air Force, but we both know that you were born with two left feet. Up until tonight.'

'Oh,' I said at a loss.

'Come on,' Peg insisted, "fess up – you've been practicing with some thin, un-pregnant cha-cha teacher on the side.' She was joking, but there was an undercurrent of tension in her words.

'Don't confuse me with Bird Dog,' I laughed, trying to ease things.

'Don't worry,' said Peg. 'The day I confuse you with Bird Dog is the day you pack your bags and move into the B.O.Q.!'

I hugged her close to me again. 'You know what?' I said.

'What?'

'I think maybe all I ever needed . . . was a well rounded partner!'

That got a smile from her, and I breathed a silent sigh of relief.

'Know what I've been thinking?' Peg asked dreamily.

'Haven't the foggiest,' I replied truthfully.

'I was thinking . . . I'd like a girl this time,' Peg said. 'How about you?'

'Oh, yeah,' I agreed, picturing a little blonde girl, a baby version of Peg. 'A girl would be nice.'

'On the other hand,' Peg continued, 'a brother for Mikey would also be good.'

'Um-hum,' I said.

The song ended, and the sweet strains of 'Friendly Persuasion' drifted from the juke box. There didn't seem to be any reason to stop dancing.

'Of course,' Peg said, 'we've got plenty of time. No matter what this one is, we'll have at least two more.'

'*What*?!' *That* startled me out of my false sense of complacency.

Peg leaned back and looked at me, surprised. 'Well, you always said you wanted to have a big family,' she told me.

'Ah . . . yeah,' I backpedalled hastily. I glanced down at her stomach and smiled. 'I guess I just wasn't thinking that far ahead, at least, not at the moment.'

'Well,' said Peg reasonably, 'of course not.' She grinned at me suddenly, a glimmer of playful sexiness showing through her smile. 'But you haven't forgotten how much fun the process is, have you?'

'Oh, no, no. Of course not,' I assured her, 'I haven't forgotten.' Jesus, I thought, a sudden surge of panic running like adrenalin through my veins, I've got to find a way out of this. I've got to!

Just then I noticed the strange technician standing inside the screen door leading to the parking lot. This guy was something else – but then, I suppose, scientists were allowed their little quirks.

He had a bright, observant look on his face, as he surveyed the smoky room. His impish face was almost . . . amused, I thought, although I wasn't certain that was precisely the right description.

He strolled casually through the dancers, right past Bird Dog and Jeannie – who were still tightly wrapped up together and oblivious to everyone around them. He didn't greet anyone. And no one greeted him either; in fact, no one even acknowledged his presence there at all. Which was peculiar, considering how he looked. He still hadn't changed out of his tuxedo, and if anything, it looked even more wrinkled than it had before; his bow tie was undone, just hanging. He couldn't have looked more out of place anywhere than he did right here.

He wandered over to the juke box, where Sally and Doug were huddled, feeding their change into the machine. They didn't appear to notice him, either.

'Peg?' I said.

'Hmmm?' She didn't bother to lift her head from its resting place on my shoulder.

'Who's the guy at the juke box?'

She half opened her eyes and raised her head to look. Then she put her head back down. 'What are you talking about? That's Doug.'

I squinted through the smoky haze of the room. I wasn't imagining things. 'No,' I said, 'I mean the guy in the tux.'

Peg didn't bother to look, she just laughed. 'A tux? In here?'

I felt a little chill run down my spine. At that moment, the technician in the tux turned and looked at me. He grinned and waved.

This was getting ridiculous. 'Come on, Peg, I'm serious. Look. You don't see a man in a tux standing over by the juke box?'

Peg cuddled closer in to me and kept her eyes closed. 'Tom,' she said softly, 'this is so nice, what's happening right now. Please don't spoil it with one of your silly pranks, okay?'

Maybe Peg just didn't really look. Or maybe someone had blocked her view. Those were the reasonable responses. But what was reasonable about this Situation? I gave myself twenty seconds to come up with an answer. Nothing. Zero. Zip.

Great, I thought. I was located somewhere in some time warp, and I was not only participating in events which had happened in the long ago past, and risking my life doing so, but on top of that, I was now seeing things that didn't even exist. I had a sudden, chilling thought. Maybe the little technician in the tux was . . . an angel of death. Or something like that. Maybe this was the goddamned Twilight Zone after all, and nothing that

63

ever happened again would ever make any sense to me at all.

I saw the technician's eyes twinkle from across the room, as if he could read my thoughts. That did it. Whatever he – it – was, I was going to find out. I turned Peg gently around and danced her across the floor to our table. Then I stepped back from her and pulled out her chair.

'Go on, honey,' I said, 'sit down.'

'Oh, Tom,' Peg's blue eyes clouded with disappointment.

I patted her gently on the shoulder. 'You're six months along,' I reminded her. 'At six months, you dance one and sit one out.'

'We danced two,' Peg reminded me with a pout. 'Two plus!'

I nodded firmly in agreement. 'That's right, and that's precisely why you're going to sit the next two out,' I said. 'Doctor's orders.'

I blinked. Something in those words – doctor's orders – rang a faint bell somewhere deep inside my mind. But it was a fleeting, visceral feeling, not really a memory at all. And try as I did, I just couldn't make it get any clearer than that.

'I really do feel fine, Tom,' Peg insisted, but it sounded more like a plea. 'And we haven't danced for so long. And you never danced so well.' She looked up at me with an expression that melted my heart. 'And I love this song.'

I picked up her hand and held it for a moment. 'I just don't want you to overdo it. We've got all night.' I smiled at her. 'Okay?'

Peg shrugged, then nodded reluctantly. 'Okay.'

I winked at her. 'I'm going to feed the old juke box – I'll be right back.'

'Play "A Blossom Fell", okay?' Peg called out after me.

'You bet,' I said. Then I summoned up every bit of courage I had, and walked across the room.

CHAPTER SEVEN

I couldn't let myself think about what I was doing; I simply propelled myself in the direction of the only person I had seen since this bizarre adventure had begun who seemed to promise even a glimmer of hope in the way of a possible explanation. By the time I wove my way between exuberant dancing couples and jovially returned a couple of slap-on-the-back greetings from relaxing flyers, the only person standing by the juke box was the object of my focus: the disappearing technician in the wrinkled tuxedo. He saluted me and grinned as I approached.

Suddenly, I was at a total loss for words. I managed a feeble smile and saluted back. 'Hey, there,' I said, for want of a better opening.

He winked, his dark little eyes sly and enquiring. Or maybe that was just my imagination. 'Hey yourself, Captain.' There was that same strange, almost questioning emphasis on the word Captain. Or was I just imagining things?

I began to feel increasingly awkward. I wasn't exactly sure how to get this conversation off to a flying start without sounding like a candidate for the men with the butterfly nets, so for the moment, I simply began to feed quarters into the juke box. I concentrated on names of tunes that rang dim bells from some long-ago past; some didn't ring any bells at all, but I did manage to locate Peg's request, 'A Blossom Fell'. It sounded vaguely familiar.

I peered across the smoky room and saw that Peg was looking in our direction, so I waved. She smiled when she heard her song begin, and then she turned to reply to something Sally was saying.

There didn't seem to be any way to delay what I felt I had to do. I took a deep breath and looked over at the technician.

He just kind of lounged in place, surveying the room with that amused look. Before I could formulate my opening sentence, however, he turned towards me with a conspiratorial smile and began to talk.

'Isn't this great?' he said enthusiastically, gesturing around the room with an expansive wave. 'Isn't this something for the books?'

I wasn't certain exactly what 'this' or what 'books' he was referring too, so I just nodded politely. 'It is . . . something, all right,' I agreed.

'Yeah,' he sighed nostalgically. 'It really does bring back the old memories, don't you think?' He turned and peered at the jukebox list. 'Hey, is "Be-Bop-A-Lula" on here?'

I shrugged helplessly. 'I didn't notice it,' I replied.

'That particular song has some very important memories attached to it,' he said.

At least he had memories to be attached to, I thought.

'Yeah, that song got me through some very long, very cold nights in the old days back at MIT,' he mused fondly. Then he grinned. ' "Be-Bop" and a little Lithuanian girl named . . . ah, Danesa, that's right. Danesa.' He savored the word; it must have been an extremely tactile recollection, judging from his expression. 'She worked in the chemistry lab, they were doing research on the effects of . . .'

I couldn't take it any more. 'I have a question,' I said, interrupting him in mid-sex recollection.

He paused, then nodded expectantly. 'I kind of thought you would by now.'

Here goes, I thought, and took a deep breath. 'Am I dead?'

'What?' He looked more than a little taken aback; that obviously wasn't the question he had been expecting to hear from me.

But there was no retreating now. 'Dead,' I repeated tenaciously. 'Am I dead?'

'Dead?' he repeated uncertainly.

I barreled on, feeling increasingly like an ass, but determined to make my point. 'It would explain a lot of things if I were dead,' I said firmly. 'I mean, I could be in a reverse kind of reincarnation that's entered in mid-life.'

'Ah . . .' He actually seemed to be at a loss for words, and I had the feeling that speechlessness was a condition in which he didn't often find himself.

'Well, I could be, couldn't I?' I persisted. Might as well be hanged – or locked away in the looney bin – for a sheep as for a lamb. Or for a psychotic as for a garden variety neurotic. Whatever. I was in too deep to extricate myself now.

But the technician didn't really look shocked by my question, at least, not shocked in the way a normal person would be shocked. He just seemed sort of . . . bemused. 'That's not bad, Sam, that's actually pretty good,' he said finally, giving me a tentative smile.

The use of the name startled me. 'What did you say?' I demanded sharply.

'Huh . . . what?' He just looked confused.

'Sam!' I repeated. I stared intently at him. 'You called me Sam! You know my name!'

The technician picked a piece of lint off his tux and studied it. He looked up, his expression a little affronted.

'Well, of course I do – I'm not *that* wasted,' he said.

This was hardly the time to discuss his degree of inebriation; I wasn't interested. 'Who *are* you?' I asked bluntly.

He stared steadily at me for a moment, as if he expected me to come up with an answer to my own question. When I didn't, he said thoughtfully, 'This is worse than I thought.'

'*What's* worse than you thought?' I demanded. 'What the hell is going on here?' I forced myself to lower my voice. 'Please tell me what's going on,' I said more softly.

'You really don't know?' he asked dubiously. 'This isn't all an act for the benefit of . . .' he gestured towards the room again.

I sighed. 'Listen to me, please, whoever you are.' I put my whole heart, all my conviction into my next statement. 'This is no act. No way. No act,' I repeated firmly.

He studied my face for any hint that I might be joking, then appeared to begin, reluctantly, to accept that this might be the truth. 'Wow,' he said, with a sigh. 'You're serious, aren't you?'

'Dead serious,' I replied. 'No pun intended, either.'

'Wow,' he said again, shaking his head.

'Let's start at the beginning,' I suggested pragmatically. 'You just called me Sam. You've *got* to tell me – who *am* I? And why is it that you know who I really am when no one else – including me – does?'

A frown creased the technician's brow. Now he looked both convinced and perturbed.

'Hey, Pard!'

I turned and saw Bird Dog grinning at me from less than a yard away, still dancing in a very friendly manner with Jeannie. I tried a smile in return, but it was probably pretty feeble looking. Good humor was not my strong point, not at the moment, at least.

Bird Dog winked at me, then shook his head sadly. 'You're really slippin', Pard.'

'Huh?' I had no idea what he was talking about. Then again, I didn't seem to have much idea what *anyone* was talking about.

'Aw, come on! No one's gonna actually fall for that old "talkin' to someone who isn't there" gag – that went out with Harry Truman!'

Although I am certain my smile got even weaker, I held onto it resolutely until he and Jeannie danced away. Then I turned back towards the technician; I hovered over the juke box, shielding my face with my bent arm, so it would appear that I was checking out the musical selections – and so it *wouldn't* look as if I was talking to anybody. Or nobody. Depending on whose point of view you happened to believe.

'Okay. So I'm a goddamned ghost,' I hissed, 'and you, apparently, are the invisible man! Am I supposed to believe that *that's* what's going on here?' I tried to keep an edge of hysteria from creeping into my voice.

'Oy vey,' said the technician. 'Sam.' He shook his head. 'I can't believe this is happening.'

'*You* can't believe it!' I exploded quietly.

'Listen to me,' he said seriously. 'Are you telling me also that you don't remember our project?' His eyes were getting somber.

'What project?' I replied through gritted teeth. 'I don't know what you're talking about. For Christ's sake, if I can't remember my name, how the hell do you expect me to remember anything *else*?'

The technician seemed to almost visibly deflate. He ran a hand across his forehead, perplexed. 'My God,' he said, more to himself than to me, 'This is terrible. That putz Ziggy was right!'

Ziggy. I felt a little jolt of recognition run up my

spine. Ziggy. An odd name, but one that somehow sounded . . . familiar. I forced myself to remain calm, to just concentrate on that name and the images it conjured up, to try to just *remember*. 'Ziggy,' I said softly, trying it out on my tongue. 'Ziggy . . . I remember a Ziggy, I think.'

'You do?' the technician said hopefully.

'Ah . . .' I strained harder for any kind of visual recollection. Something seemed to click, and I got a very faint picture in my mind. 'Ziggy. Ziggy,' I repeated, as if just the mere act of repetition would bring it all back to me. It didn't work. 'Nothing,' I said, frustrated.

The technician sighed. I could tell I had disappointed him.

I fought back a pang of my own panicked disappointment. 'What . . . what *now*?' I demanded.

'Oh, come *on*, Tom, this is gettin' ridiculous,' Bird Dog laughed as he twirled Jeannie by me again. 'Everyone at the table's takin' bets on when you're gonna give up and admit that this one just isn't workin'!'

I turned to look across the room, and sure enough, Doug, Sally and Peg were all looking my way. Doug and Sally were laughing as they gestured towards me and my invisible pal, and I was momentarily grateful for my – Tom's – reputation as a relentless practical joker; but then, even through the haze, I could see that Peg looked a little anxious, and I felt a pang of guilt for worrying her. But then, I had my own problems to worry about. I smiled at her as reassuringly as I could, then turned back to the technician.

He was gone.

No, I thought, please, the panic now really surfacing, please don't let this be happening! I was just starting to get somewhere. I had the sudden thought that perhaps he was just invisible to me, now, the way he seemed to be to everyone else all the time.

'Hey,' I said softly, masking my mouth with my hand, as if I was coughing. 'Hey, are you here?'

Silence greeted my efforts. 'Hey,' I said again, hoping against hope.

But there was no reply, no sound at all except the strains of Elvis emanating from the juke box. I had to restrain myself from pounding on it in sheer frustration.

I took a deep breath to steady my nerves. I had to think clearly. I had to figure out exactly what to do now. I felt a toughening, a stubborn determination welling up inside me, overriding the panic. And then I knew there was no way I was going to let this little man – if, indeed, that was even what he really was – just slip away from me. He knew things I desperately needed to know, not the least of which was my real identity. So it followed logically, if anything in this bizarre new world followed logically, that he must know where I came from, how I got here. *Why* I was here. He couldn't be allowed to just . . . leave! He had to answer my questions.

I looked rapidly around the room, but there was no trace of him. Then I saw the screen door bang closed behind emptiness. I didn't stop to think, I just acted on instinct and headed for the door, somehow certain that he had left. Determinedly avoiding what I was sure would be the troubled look on Peg's face if she noticed my departure, I hurriedly elbowed my way through the growing crowd. I reached the screen door and pushed through it. Outside, I glanced both ways, from one end of the rough wooden porch to the other. He was nowhere to be seen. But I was certain he was there, somewhere.

I raced to the end of the porch, and quickly surveyed the large dirt parking lot from there. It was filled with vintage cars parked at haphazard, crazy angles – two-tone Chevys, Ford pick-ups with grinning-tooth grills, rocketship-like Oldsmobiles. In them were, no doubt, necking couples, and as I stood there in the relative quiet, I could hear faint strains of the jukebox music floating out into the soft night air. If this scene had been in a movie, it would have been an endearingly nostalgic scene, but there was nothing even remotely endearing about it to me.

After a quick assessing look around, I leapt off the end of the veranda and down into the dusk of the parking lot. I made my way steadily between the parked cars, searching for some sign of the technician, the one person who held the key to the secret of my life as it now was. Nothing.

There was nowhere else left to go, so I headed towards the edge of the highway and peered off into the dark distance. It was empty in both directions, just a black-topped two-lane road stretching through the middle of the high desert in the quiet night. Above me, the inky black sky was dotted with brilliant stars and a pale sliver of crescent moon. The vague outline of the mountains beyond the Mojave were just barely visible in the eerie night. Suddenly, I caught a faint motion out of the corner of my eye.

I whipped around just in time to see the technician disappearing again. But this time it was different – this time I could actually see him go. He appeared to be opening an invisible panel in the atmosphere, a non-existent doorway leading him into some place, some time, other than this one. I saw him gaze quickly back at me, and I thought there was compassion in that look; then he pulled the panel shut behind him.

I shook my head as if to clear it, and looked again. there was nothing but what had been before – the empty desert, the distant mountains, the blacktop, the enigmatic dark sky stretching to infinity above and around me.

There was no strange technician, no invisible doorway to the beyond. No doorway for me, that is.

The darkness, the silence, the seeming inevitability of my predicament suddenly overwhelmed me, and I sank down onto my knees by the side of the highway, burying my face in my hands.

I was insane.

I was hallucinating.

I was trapped.

I raised my face from my hands and stared at the stars twinkling coldly and inaccessibly above me.

'Please God,' I said softly, 'I'd like to wake up now.'

CHAPTER EIGHT

It took every ounce of inner strength I had in reserve –
and then some I didn't know I possessed – to drag myself
to my feet, brush the dirt off my pants, and force myself
to return to the loud, gratingly cheerful atmosphere
inside the Ranch. Although I felt my façade was paper-
thin, I tried my best to keep a pleasant, unconcerned
expression on my face as I approached the table where
Peg and the Walkers were deep in gossipy conversation.

'Where'd *you* go?' asked Doug.

'Just outside for a minute,' I replied with a shrug. 'It's
so smoky in here, I felt like I needed a breath of fresh
air.'

'You okay, honey?' Peg asked, concerned. 'You have a
headache or something?'

'No, I'm fine,' I assured her, and slid into the chair
next to hers.

'Personally,' Sally Walker returned to the topic at hand
with a sly little grin, 'for all his big talk, I think that Bird
Dog may be the one who finds himself hog-tied this time.'

I sort of eased off into myself as the three of them
chattered about Bird Dog's romantic entanglements,
and whether or not this particular blonde might be *the*
blonde who would actually succeed in getting the laconic
and elusive Texas bachelor to hang up his stetson
permanently. It seemed to be an ongoing topic of conversation among the flyers' wives, complete with a
betting pool. I just nodded and gave the occasional
obligatory 'uh-huh,' while my mind went over what had

happened with the technician, again and again. There was no logical explanation for it, not his appearance or his disappearance, not his cryptic questions and hints; but then again, I asked myself, why would I expect there to be? There was no logical explanation for any of this.

Except . . . perhaps, my own spur of the moment theory about reverse reincarnation, which had seemed to perk the technician's interest. But I had no idea where that theory had sprung from, and try as I might, I couldn't make myself take it any further. I sighed.

'Are you sure you're all right, Tom?'

Peg's question brought me back from my reverie. 'I'm sure,' I said. 'How about a last dance, then we blow this pop stand?'

'Blow this pop stand . . .' Peg looked puzzled, then she smiled and shrugged. 'A dance with the new Gene Kelly sounds good to me.'

'Love Is a Many Splendored Thing' didn't require much dancing skill – just sort of standing in one place and swaying; so I was spared Peg's inquiries about just where I had learned to dance. She felt so good in my arms, so real. She smelled like spring flowers, and I held onto her as the one tangible thing I could rely on in this new life. It wasn't fair, perhaps, but for the moment, it was the only comfort I could find. I assuaged my guilty conscience by reminding myself that Peg had no idea the man she was dancing with wasn't really Tom. And after all, it wasn't as if I was taking advantage of the situation. Not really. I felt Peg sigh, her head nestled softly against my shoulder.

'Tired?' I asked.

'A little,' she admitted, looking up at me with shining blue eyes, 'but I'm having so much fun, I don't want this night to end.'

'Still,' I said pragmatically, leading her off the floor, 'I think it's time you got some rest.'

'Oh, okay, boss,' she said with a smiling kind of a pout that I found adorable.

Peg retrieved her cardigan from the chair, and we said our goodnights to everyone there. Bird Dog was back, watching Tony dance with Jeannie again. Despite the speculative gossip about his imminent fall from bachelorhood, he didn't seem particularly perturbed by the sight of the two of them twirling around the dance floor. He winked at me as Peg and I turned to leave.

'Don't forget about Monday, Pard.'

I smiled uneasily. 'No chance,' I said. As if I *could* forget about it.

I looked around for seatbelts when Peg and I got back into the '56 Chevy, then remembered again that there weren't any.

'What do you keep looking for?' asked Peg with a sleepy yawn. I had done the same thing earlier that evening, when we were setting out.

'Ah . . . I think I dropped a screwdriver between the seats when I was adjusting . . .' I let the words trail off. What did you adjust on this monolithic car, with its round rocketship dashboard dials and shift lever on the steering column? For distraction, I reached over and switched on the radio.

It was Frank Sinatra singing 'The Tender Trap', and Peg sighed happily. 'Oh, I just love this song,' she said contentedly.

I concentrated on my driving. There were no lights on this black desert highway, and the oil-covered center stripe had almost faded into the blacktop. It was extremely difficult to see, hard to tell where the pavement ended and the sand began. Only an occasional yucca tree, its branches outlined dark against the darker sky, indicated the demarcation between desert and blacktop.

My mind drifted. 'I never realized how hard it was to follow a road without striping,' I said.

'Striping?' Peg said, puzzled. 'What's that?'

Oh, Jesus, I had done it again. I glanced quickly over at her, but she just looked perplexed, not at all suspicious.

'Oh,' I improvised hastily, 'it's just something I was thinking about. You know, if they painted white stripes along the sides of the road, that would make it easier to see at night.'

Peg was silent for a moment, peering out into the darkness ahead. 'That's a really good idea, Tom,' she said finally. She seemed a little surprised by my inventive suggestion.

I bit back an ironic smile: now *here* was an easy way to make people think I was brilliant – just stick around in 1956 and come up with ideas that I knew were going to happen in the future. 'I've got a few of them,' I admitted. Right. Just call me the new Thomas Edison.

Peg smiled at me, then she slid across the slick vinyl of the big bench seat and snuggled up against me, laying her head on my shoulder. It made me feel good. It made me feel guilty. It made me feel like . . . a teenager.

'Tonight was so much fun,' Peg said. The way she said it, kind of wistfully, made me wonder if the real Tom ever took any time to have fun with his lovely wife.

'Good,' I said. 'I thought so, too.'

'But you know what?'

Uh-oh, I thought. 'What?'

'It was also . . . I don't know, a little scary.' Peg sounded tentative.

'Scary?' I said. 'Why scary?'

I could feel her shrug. 'I don't know, exactly.' She thought about it for a moment. 'Maybe because . . . you wanted to dance,' she said.

'It's not the first time we danced,' I said, hoping I wasn't stepping into a colossal blunder.

'I know,' said Peg.

Whew.

'But it was just ... different. I mean, *you* were different.'

Uh-oh again. 'I was?' I said.

'Well, you didn't drink more than one or two beers all night,' Peg continued, toting up Tom's strange new behavior in her head. 'And ... you didn't talk flying.' She stared over at me. 'And I can't *ever* remember a time when we were at a table full of pilots and you didn't talk about airplanes.'

I sighed. 'It seems to me that that's *all* we talked about.'

'No, that's all *they* talked about,' Peg corrected me.

Of course, she was right – how could I contribute to a conversation about a subject I didn't know anything about. I had listened and nodded, but I hadn't said a word.

'You didn't say a word.' Peg echoed my thoughts aloud.

She was too damned observant, I thought ruefully. But I liked her all the better for it – smart, sweet, pretty. 'I guess I just wasn't in a very talkative mood, that's all,' I told her with a dismissive shrug.

'You were when you were at the juke box,' Peg said softly, and I wondered if this was where she had been leading the conversation, right from the start.

I was trying to formulate a response when a convenient distraction appeared. The beams of the Chevy's head-lights picked out a roadside sign.

'Why is it ...' I read.

Peg saw it too, and sat up, reading off the next sign along with me, '... when you ...'

A third sign flashed by. '... try to pass ...' we read.

The fourth brightened and disappeared. '... the guy in front ...'

79

Fifth. 'goes twice as fast,' we read in tandem, then, chorused along with the last sign, 'Burma Shave!'

Peg looked at me and we laughed, as the vision of the last sign flashed by and disappeared. She reached up and stroked my cheek gently. 'Feels good,' she said. 'How did you like it?'

'Better than my electric razor,' I replied without thinking.

Peg's smile vanished, and she moved away from me, leaning back against the passenger door. She stared at me with somber eyes.

'I . . . don't use an electric razor, do I?' I finally said.

'No,' said Peg. 'You don't.' She studied my face for a long moment. 'Tom,' she said, 'what's going on?'

I sighed. 'I wish I knew.' The words came out unbidden.

'Tom, please,' Peg said, worry and impatience mixing in her tone. 'Just tell me.'

I felt trapped. Trapped by everything, not just this time and this place, but by my own confusion, by words that came out when I didn't mean them to. Words that somehow had to be explained. Finally, I ventured, 'What if I told you my name wasn't really Tom?'

Peg looked bewildered. 'What do you mean? You said that this morning.'

I took a deep breath. 'I know. It's Sam. Not Tom. My name, that is.'

'Sam?' she echoed hollowly.

'Uh-huh. But don't ask me my last name, because I can't remember it.' I pulled the rear view mirror down to an angle where I could see my reflection – Tom's reflection – in it. 'And when I look in the mirror, I don't know who I'm looking at. Tom Stratton, I guess. But he's not me.' The words just came tumbling out, a rapid-fire confession. 'And I can't fly. In fact, I don't know what I *can* do. I don't know who I am, or why I'm here.' Frustrated, I pushed the mirror back into place. Then I glanced quickly over at Peg for her reaction, and saw her shrink back against the door, her eyes misting.

'Tom . . .' she said tremulously.

But I had started – I felt I *had* to continue, consequences be damned. 'No. Peg, listen to what I'm telling you, I'm *not* Tom Stratton. When I woke up this morning, I didn't know where I was. I didn't know you or Mikey or anyone on the base.' I took a deep breath. 'I know I must sound like I belong in a looney bin, but I swear, it's the truth.'

'Tom . . .'

I barrelled on. 'Peg, the reason I'm acting different is because I *am* different. I know how crazy this must sound, but you have to believe me – I'm *not* your Tom.'

I looked quickly over at her again. Tears were pouring down her face. I had forgotten how sensitive pregnant women were . . .

'Please don't cry,' I said softly.

Peg gave a hiccuping kind of a sob. 'Then stop doing this to me!'

I felt helpless. 'But you asked me to explain . . .'

She sobbed harder. 'Stop it!' she said, an edge of hysteria in her voice, 'Just stop it, Tom! This isn't funny!'

The idea of consequences be damned flew right out the window when I saw the genuine pain I was causing. I felt like a heel of the cruelest sort. Why was I doing this. How could she believe me? How could I expect this woman to accept, to understand something which utterly baffled me? And what would I gain from this confession? Nothing, I concluded. Nothing at all.

I reached gently over and touched her on the shoulder, a gesture of apology. But Peg jerked back from my touch as if I had stung her. And I couldn't blame her, either. I couldn't stand it any more, the way I was hurting her, and I had to back off. Just be . . . good old Tom, that silly practical joker.

'Peg, I'm sorry,' I said contritely. 'I don't know what's come over me . . .'

'What are you *doing?*' she demanded. 'What in God's name has gotten into you – this is so cruel!'

I couldn't have felt any more despicable. 'I'm sorry,' I repeated humbly. 'I'm being a complete nerd, and I apologize.'

Peg looked at me with reproachful, teary eyes. I couldn't believe it – she even looked pretty crying. 'I just don't understand,' she said. 'What on earth is this all about?'

On earth – hah! Good phrase, good question. 'Well . . .' I improvised hastily. 'You were right, honey. I'm setting up a gag.'

She sighed with relief. 'Well, thank God for that. You had me frightened half to death.'

God, I felt like such a jerk. 'I'm sorry, honey, I shouldn't have tried it on you.'

Peg wiped her eyes. 'I swear, Tom, you just don't know what a good actor you are. You had me halfway convinced you had a brain tumor or something.'

'Hmm,' I said thoughtfully, 'that's an interesting idea. I never thought of that.'

'What?' said Peg. 'What do you mean you never thought of that?' She was beginning to look worried again.

I had to learn to keep my mouth shut, I thought. 'Oh, you know, it's just that Bird Dog and I have been dreaming up theories to explain why I can't fly – a brain tumor is a pretty good explanation.' I glanced over at her, and she looked relaxed again. 'See, that's the gag, we tell Weird Ernie that I can't remember how to fly.'

82

'You can't fly?' Peg almost giggled.

'Uh-huh,' I said, pretending to warm to my subject. 'We really got him going this morning – everyone said they couldn't remember something – their car, their wife's birthday – that was Doug, by the way – after they reached a certain speed.'

'Oh, you didn't,' Peg said.

'Oh, we did,' I assured her. 'Weird Ernie even asked Dr Burger to work up some sort of test to check this all out.'

Peg laughed again. 'You . . . not being able to fly.' She looked fondly over at me. 'Tom, that's got to be the dumbest thing I ever heard.'

'Oh, I don't know,' I said thoughtfully. 'It sounds pretty plausible to me.'

'You silly thing.' Peg's equilibrium seemed perfectly restored.

'Uh-huh,' I said. 'That's me.'

Peg opened the glove compartment and rummaged around until she found some Kleenex. She blew her nose and fussed with her hair. Then she slid back across the bench seat and put her head on my shoulder again. It felt so good, so comforting. I sighed and put my arm around her shoulder.

The blacktop sped by, and the miles passed, while we drove in silence, the only sound the music coming from the radio.

Finally, Peg broke the silence. 'Tom?' she said.

'What, honey?'

'What's a nerd?' she asked innocently.

I couldn't help it, I just started to laugh. It was quite a relief, too.

CHAPTER NINE

The rest of the drive home was uneventful. Peg seemed to recover. She chattered away about Bird Dog and his flirtation, about how Tony was taking it, about Sally and Doug's nervousness about her pregnancy. Regular, everyday conversation between married people. I guess. I wondered if, back in that world that I came from, that world I couldn't remember, I was married. Had children. Had normal, familiar conversations like this.

Back at the house, however, Peg did give me a startled look when I offered to drive the sullen – and now sleepy – babysitter home.

'It's just five houses from here, Tom,' she reminded me.

I shrugged foolishly. 'I know that,' I protested, 'but you can't be too careful these days.'

Peg gave me another peculiar look. 'There's nothing around here to be careful about,' she protested. Then she smiled. 'What are you doing, practicing up in case we do have a daughter?'

I just nodded and shrugged and thought to myself, by the time that baby girl grows up, you won't be half so sanguine about letting teenaged girls out at night. But we settled on my walking Judy two houses up the block, and watching her the rest of the way, until I could see that she had let herself safely into her house.

We got ready for bed, Peg changing modestly into her baby dolls in the bathroom. Thank Heavens, I thought again, for her advanced state of pregnancy. Lust was one problem I didn't have to deal with. At least, not unless I got stuck here for another couple of months, and I just couldn't let myself think that might happen. So I pulled on Tom's pajama bottoms and climbed into bed.

Sam, I thought, my name is Sam. Well, it was a starting point, anyway. But Sam what? I tried as hard as I could to conjure up a last name to go with Sam, but it simply wouldn't come. So I switched gears and tried to picture myself – my real self, Sam – in any situation that might jog my memory: at the grocery store, in an office, crossing the street, lying in bed like I was right now. Nothing.

'Tom?' Peg said enquiringly as she slid into bed beside me.

'Huh?'

'Why are you squinting like that?'

'Like what?' I said.

'I don't know, you had your face all scrunched up like you were thinking really hard about something.' She imitated me, wrinkling up her pretty face until it resembled a prune. 'Like this.'

'Did I?' I asked innocently.

'Yes.'

I shrugged.

Peg stared inquiringly at me, then shrugged too. She switched off the light. 'Well, it was fun tonight, but maybe you're right about taking it a little easier. I'm bushed.' She gave me a gentle kiss on the cheek. 'Good night, honey,' she said. 'Sweet dreams.'

Right. Sweet dreams in a strange bed with a strange wife in a strange world. Sure. No problem. No memory, but what the hell? No problem. 'You too,' I replied, thinking it would be a long and restless night.

But to my surprise, it wasn't very long at all before I dropped off into a heavy sleep; it must have been pure emotional exhaustion setting in, telling my brain, Tom's or Sam's or somebody's brain, anyway, that it needed some serious rest.

Then I began to dream. It was similar to the dreams I'd had the night before: I was suspended somewhere in space and time, and suddenly, out of a blank blue expanse of sky, clouds roiled and rushed by me in fast-forward motion. Great black and purple plumes of clouds, surreal and huge, moved rapid-fire across an endless, dark horizon, while I just stared and stared. Then, without warning, I took off, launched upwards like a one-man rocket into deep space. As I rushed easily by the clouds, I looked down. Somehow, in dream logic, the sky had become perfectly clear again, and I could see Tom and Peg's house, the street full of similar houses, growing smaller and smaller beneath me.

My view expanded as I rose, and there was the entire air base spread below me, the street where the houses were now just a faint curved line on this strange visual topography. The dry lake bed – a large, irregular brown splotch – joined the visual map, and soon, I could see every place I had been that day mapped out below. Then it all receded, becoming just a vague series of dots in a vast, unending desert . . .

I seemed to slow in my upward flight, to hang suspended in the air again, unmoving for a moment. Then I saw the clouds again, first a wispy tendril approaching by itself, and then a huge, rolling bank of them. I was surrounded, enveloped in a mist-like mass, and then, as suddenly as I had risen, I began a stomach-turning plummet back to earth. Faster and faster, I fell by the clouds, saw the topography below me clear and separate into the various now-familiar locations . . .

I could see the house, the Stratton's house, rushing up at me, and then there was a Boom!

'Ah!' My eyes popped open, and I woke up.

It was almost an exact replay of the morning before. I was still here in the Stratton's house, and I had no doubt that I still looked like Tom Stratton. But now, I reminded myself in my half-awake state, I had more information . . . I knew my name.

'Honey,' Peg rolled over sleepily, half opening her eyes.

'Hmmm?' I said, distracted.

'What . . .'

I recovered myself quickly. 'Nothing, Peg, it's nothing. Just go back to sleep.'

She was tired enough to take my words at face value, and she rolled back in the other direction. Her breathing became regular again, and then I took a deep breath myself and exhaled slowly. Some dream, I thought. I slid back down on the pillow, tugged at the light blanket, and tried to make myself comfortable. Relax, I told myself, just relax. There was nothing else to do – it was the middle of the night.

But the dream troubled me, and I kept replaying it in my head. I felt as if it must be tied into my experiences, my present state, but I couldn't make the connection. Okay, I told myself, take ten deep breaths. Concentrate on relaxing your body, part by part, starting at the toes. Of course, I had no idea how I knew to do this, but I was beginning to trust my instincts, to believe that going on instinct might be the one thing that would begin to jar my memory.

By the time I had worked my way up to my fingertips, I could feel my heart beat slowing. That is all I need, I thought, a good night's sleep. I started to drift. No sense in mulling things over in an insomniac state – I would figure it all out in the morning, when I got up to milk the cows.

My eyes popped back open. Milk the cows? Where had that come from?

I sat quietly up and concentrated. This time, something finally happened. I broke through some barrier in my own mind, and suddenly, I could remember that I had been raised on a dairy farm in the Midwest . . . in, ah, in Indiana! I remembered it with a feeling of triumph. I could almost see it, all green and pastoral. In, ah, a little town called . . . Elk's Grove. No, Elk's Ridge. I felt a surge of adrenalin and hope rush through me. Okay, I told myself, it's happening. Keep going.

I was raised on a dairy farm in Elk's Grove until I was eighteen, and then I left to go to college at . . . at . . . Ah, shit! I went absolutely blank. I glanced over at Peg sleeping peacefully, and realized I had better take myself and my newfound memory out of bed, out of the room: if anything substantial came back to me, I was likely to start bouncing off the walls!

I pulled on a robe and padded quietly out of the bedroom. I headed for the refrigerator and poured myself a glass of milk. It felt cold and reminiscent going down – milk, childhood. I forced myself to remain focused on childhood – I had lost track when I tried to remember as far as college.

I stared out the kitchen window, watching the black sky begin to fade into very early dawn. A farm, I was raised on a farm with my . . . sister! Kate! Katie was older than me, and she married a naval officer of some sort. A . . . lieutenant named John. No, that was wrong. Not John, but something like it. Jim. Jim Bellows. I sighed a deep sigh of satisfaction. That was right, and I could actually remember someone's last name, if not . . . my own.

'All right,' I congratulated myself softly. 'All damned right!'

There had to be more. I forced myself to think, to try

to visualize. I could see the rows of placid, black and white Guernsey cows, neatly housed in clean stalls, hear their gentle lowing as we approached; I could almost smell the pungent odors of fresh hay and sweet, warm milk as I urged it from their udders into the waiting tin pails. I could feel the milking stool I sat on. And I could see Katie, but she was dim and distant. That was okay – at least she was there.

Katie and Jim Bellows. I knew their *names*, I thought, a feeling of incredible joy sweeping over me. I could *find* them. Let's see. Jim was stationed somewhere in Hawaii, that was right. And Mom – Mom! – lived with them. Since . . . Dad . . .

'Oh, my God,' I said, a shock wave washing over me as this memory flooded back.

Since Dad died in 1974. My Dad had died in 1974 of a massive coronary. I wasn't there . . . that much I knew. I couldn't remember any more, just a feeling of overwhelming loss and sadness. And regret. For what? For an estrangement? I had no idea, and that was the saddest thing of all.

But, I thought with a sudden surge of renewed hope, this was 1956. My father was still *alive*. I sagged back against the linoleum counter. Was it, could it really be possible? Could I reach my father in the past – now – and talk to him? I was dazed by the idea of it, and somehow, I knew instinctively that if I could reach him, I could say things to him that I probably never said when he was alive. Things I should have told him.

I could feel my heart rate increase, my palms begin to sweat. The very idea was so outrageous, so . . . otherworldly. Contrary to any kind of acceptable belief. But . . . so was the fact of my being here. Could you talk to the dead, I wondered? Could you rectify past mistakes? Did I dare even try?

I gazed out the window again, then over at the enameled kitchen wall clock. Five twenty. This was the time the farm came awake. Dad would be up.

I walked slowly into the living room, approaching the phone tentatively, as if it were a living creature. It stood, black, shiny, a challenge to every normal concept of reality. I picked up the receiver gingerly, and, holding my breath, dialed O.

'Operator.' Her voice was hoarse and nasal, but not unfriendly.

I closed my eyes and thought, here goes. 'Operator,' I said firmly, 'I'd like long distance.'

'Just a moment, please, I'll connect you with the long distance operator.'

There was a click on the line, and then another voice came on. 'Long distance operator. Where are you calling?'

'Indiana,' I said. 'Elk Ridge, Indiana.'

Then it hit me: I didn't know who I was calling in Elk Ridge. I gasped.

'What number, please.'

I felt the breath being sucked out of me. 'Uh . . .' I tried desperately to remember, but my mind was an absolute blank.

'What number, please,' repeated the disembodied voice patiently.

'I don't know . . .' I said faintly.

'Sir . . .'

I squeezed my eyes shut. 'I'm trying to remember, operator. It's just that it's been a long time . . .'

'Sir . . .'

'No, wait!' I said pleadingly. A name leaped into my mind. 'Oakdell. It was, ah . . . Oakdell.'

'Sir, Oakdell what?'

'I don't know,' I said despairingly. 'I just don't know!'

The operator paused. She must have heard the desperation in my voice, because when she spoke again, her voice was gentler, more personal somehow. 'Sir,' she said, 'why don't you just give me the name of the party you wish to contact in Elk Ridge, and I'll get the number for you from their local information.'

'I . . .' my voice was cracking.

'Sir?'

The chance of a lifetime. A deathtime. Whatever this was, I was going to lose the opportunity to talk to my father, just once more. Just because I couldn't remember the goddamned number.

'Sir?' she repeated. 'Do you wish me to try Elk Ridge information?'

I pulled the receiver away from my ear, and, tears sliding unexpectedly down my cheeks, hung the phone gently up. I don't think I could ever have felt so completely alone in the universe, so abandoned. So sad.

'Dad?'

The tentative little voice startled me. I looked up to see Mikey hovering hesitantly in the doorway to the hall, watching me. He had a frightened expression on his round, freckled face. I wondered how long he had been there, how much he had heard.

'Dad, what's wrong?'

I blundered back into the kitchen, grabbed a paper towel, and hastily wiped the tears from my face.

Mikey had followed me. 'Are you getting sick or something?'

What a good idea, I thought. I blew my nose, making a great show of it. 'I think I might be catching a cold,' I said.

'I thought so,' said Mikey, happy with this acceptable explanation, 'you sound kind of funny.'

Not half as funny as.I feel, I thought.

'Uh, Dad?'

'Yes,' I said.

'Do you want to skip the fishing trip, if you're sick, I mean?'

'What?'

Mikey stared at me with clear, innocent eyes. 'You didn't forget, did you? It's Saturday. You said we could go fishing today.' He looked at me, concerned. 'But you know, we don't really have to if you don't feel good.'

He was a sweet, thoughtful kid. Peg was a sweet, thoughtful woman. Oh, God, what was I going to do about all this?

I looked at Mikey standing there in his too-small Davey Crockett pajamas, with one of those ridiculous coonskin caps perched on his crewcut. He was just an innocent kid caught up in something he would never understand – hopefully, wouldn't ever know about. All he wanted was a couple of hours with the father who was probably too busy to spend much time with him, except on those rare weekend occasions like this. I felt a pang for him and the father who wasn't there, not really, anyway.

Well, I thought, I suppose if I can't get through to my own dad, if I can't be the son I would like to be to my father, I might as well act the good father to a son who was missing his own.

I looked at him and gave him a big smile. 'What are you talking about? Don't you know that nothing cures a cold faster and better than a fishing trip?'

Mikey's smile in return was worth it all. 'Oh, boy!' he said happily. 'Come on, let's get dressed and get started. You know what you always say about getting there early while the fish are still biting.'

And he was gone in a flash of kid energy, off to get dressed and collect his gear.

'Is that what I always say?' I wondered aloud to the empty room. 'Aren't I clever?'

CHAPTER TEN

Mikey and I played a game on our way to going fishing.

'Okay, Mikey,' I said, 'now that you're . . .' Then I stopped, stumped, because, of course, I didn't exactly *know* how old he was. So I amended my opening statement quickly: 'Now that you're old enough to really get a sense of direction, let's see if you can get us to the . . . fishing spot without getting lost.'

Mikey seemed to think this was a swell idea. 'Like practicing for when I can drive?' he said eagerly.

'Exactly,' I nodded.

Pleased with this new, adult task, Mikey concentrated on the road, a serious frown creasing his little face. 'Okay,' he said, 'when we get to the first junction, we make a left turn, then we follow Old Hills Road all the way up to the pass . . .'

He was good. Even better, he was correct. He navigated us right to 'our' favorite spot at our favorite mountain stream – a remote place, quiet in the way that only places devoid of the sounds of cars can be quiet.

'Boy, this is nice,' I remarked, as we got our gear from the trunk.

'You mean you feel better?' Mikey asked innocently.

It took me a split second to remember what he was talking about, then I nodded. 'I sure do,' I said. Of course, I felt like a horse's ass in hip high rubber waders and one of those dopey canvas hats with colorful fishing flies pinned all around the brim, but at least none of it seemed terribly unfamiliar to me. Whoever Sam was – I was – I must have gone fishing at some point in my life. Probably back on the farm, I thought, and fought down a sudden moment of sadness at the memory of that attempt to reach into my own past.

'Come on, Dad,' Mikey urged me, as he waded fearlessly into the shallow waters of the rushing stream. I watched him go, cowboy hat set firmly on his brown hair, serious as he could be, and I felt an unexpected surge of pride on Tom's behalf.

Then I gathered my courage and waded in after him. We stood side by side, two fisherman buddies, surveying the rushing waters. Mikey looked up enquiringly at me. It was obvious I was supposed to kick this venture off.

I cleared my throat and faked it, hoping some sort of vague subconscious fisherman's memory would rise up and save me. I pulled my arm back, then flicked the line lightly out, towards midstream, aiming to drift it through a fast rill and into a placid pool. I winced as the fly promptly hit an eddy, and then frenziedly whipped into a tangle of driftwood. Mikey looked up at me.

'Heh-heh,' I said, 'I did that on purpose. That was just to show you what you *shouldn't* do.' I paused, trying to hide my efforts to gently tug the line free; it didn't seem to be working. 'Now, watch this,' I said, yanking. 'I'm just going to bring it back, and then I'll show you how to do it right.'

I pretended to know exactly what I was doing as I reeled the fly in part of the way. But not for long: it snagged on the wood, coming to a dead stop and pulling my line taut.

I looked at Mikey seriously and said, 'Remember, Mikey, even your best fly fisherman will get his fly snagged now and then. The trick is not to get impatient.' I struggled valiantly to work the damned thing free. 'It's the old pro who can work it free without the line . . .'

Snapping. I stared glumly at the fly, nestled across the stream in the driftwood.

'Can I try now, Dad?'

I didn't even have time to answer before Mikey, with apparent ease and the expertise of a born fly-fisherman, flicked his dry fly across the stream, landing it perfectly at the head of the pool.

I smiled gamely and patted him on the head. 'Very good, very good. Ah . . . why don't you go ahead and work this pool . . . I'll just go . . . fish further up the stream.'

I turned and began to wade – lumber is a better description, actually – through the shallow stream towards the bank.

'Dad?'

It took me a moment to realize Mikey was calling me. I guess 'dad' wasn't something I was used to being called.

'Yeah?' I said, turning.

Mikey smiled at me. 'I know what you're doing,' he said.

I didn't. 'What's that?' I asked apprehensively.

'I know you're just trying to make me look good.'

I just smiled and shook my head, then clambered up onto the bank. I stood there for a moment, watching Mikey expertly retrieving and casting his fly, all his concentration on his task. Then I turned and headed upstream. At least, I figured it was upstream, and I figured that was the way to go.

I pushed my way through thick brush, breathing in the fragrance of the eucalyptus and manzanita and scrub oak that lined the fast running stream. Eventually, I saw another likely fishing spot, a clearing with a few placid pools among the rushing waters.

What the hell? I figured. It was as good a place as any to relax and be alone with my scattered thoughts. I waded back into the water and began to very inexpertly tie a fly.

'Is that a Ginger Quill spentwing?' someone asked.

Startled, I spun around so quickly I nearly lost my footing. The disappearing technician was back again standing right beside me. He was out of his tuxedo now, wearing a brightly patterned shirt and loose jacket. Dark glasses hid his eyes, and in his hands was a clipboard with reams of computer printouts on it.

'What the hell . . . ?'

He peered at the fly. 'Or a Blue Dun?' He shook his head. 'I'm so damned hungover it could be a Coors pop top.'

This time, he wasn't going to get away. I lunged clumsily at him and grabbed . . . air. My hand literally passed through the man's body.

'Ahhhh!' I screamed, leaping back.

The technician grabbed his head. 'Don't yell!' he yelled. 'Please,' he added more quietly.

I felt all the strain of the past twenty-four hours rise up in me. I was on the edge of freaking, of bolting, of anything. I forced myself to take three deep breaths, then faced him.

'Who *are* you?' I demanded.

'A man with a king-sized headache,' he replied. 'Jesus, I should have stayed in bed with Tina, had some Alka Seltzer, ordered in a salsa omelette, something like that.' He paused, staring at me. 'You still don't remember me?' he asked.

I shook my head.

The technician sighed. 'That's sad, pal, very sad.' He sighed again. 'My name is Albert. Albert *what*, don't ask, I can't tell you that. That's restricted information. Actually, most of what you'll want to know is probably restricted information. So . . . it'll be much easier on both of us if you kind of restrict yourself and don't ask a lot of questions.'

'Don't ask a lot of questions?' I echoed in disbelief. 'You've got to be kidding!' I stared hard at him. '*What* are you?'

He wagged his finger at me. 'That's a question, Sam.' He thought about it. 'But it's one I can answer. I'm a man, just like you.'

'Just like me?' I said. Then I forced myself to reach forward and try to touch him again. It happened again: my hand passed clean through Albert's body. 'No,' I said with a shudder, 'not just like me.'

The technician waved a dismissive hand over the general vicinity of his body. 'Oh, *this* isn't me,' he said matter of factly. 'This is a phantasmic manifestation of me created by a sub-atomic agitation of carbon quarks tuned to the mesons of your optic and otic neurons.'

'Oh,' I said, with sudden, unexpected comprehension, 'you're a neurological hologram!'

He nodded happily.

'An image only I can see . . . and hear,' I continued cautiously.

The technician, Albert, really brightened at that. 'You *haven't* forgotten everything!'

I blinked. 'No,' I said, 'I guess I haven't. But I have absolutely no idea how I knew what that – what I just said.'

That took the wind out of his sails. He seemed to sag with defeat. Then he shook himself, and got right back to business. He consulted the reams of paper before him, leafing rapidly through them until he got to the one he wanted.

'Okay,' he said briskly, running his finger down the printout, 'now, Ziggy's worked up five different scenarios that might explain why we . . .'

'Ziggy,' I interrupted him, trying to recall the image that name had conjured up when we were standing at the jukebox, right before Bird Dog had danced by blowing the whole scene. 'The little guy with bad breath,' I said.

'That's Gooshie,' the technician corrected me. 'He programs Ziggy.'

'Programs . . .' I repeated slowly. It rang a faint bell in my mind.

'Ziggy's a hybrid computer,' he explained impatiently. It was obviously something I was supposed to know.

I thought about that for a moment, a bit of my memory bouncing back again. 'Hybrid computers and neurological holograms didn't exist in 1956,' I told him.

'Only in theory,' he agreed.

'But this *is* 1956, right?' I insisted.

He made a *comme ci-comme ça* gesture with his hand. 'For you. Yes.'

Oh, great. For me. This was just getting more confusing. I tried to get back on a more straightforward track. 'Okay, we can put that on the back burner for the moment, and get to basics. What's my last name?'

The technician looked at me the way a teacher looks at a recalcitrant child. 'If you don't remember, I can't tell you,' he said.

'That's ridiculous!' I exclaimed.

'Why?'

'Why? I don't know why!' I said through clenched teeth. 'Because . . . it's *important* for me to know my last name, that's why!'

The technician pursed his lips. 'It's also right at the top of Ziggy's no-no list. Double starred,' he added seriously.

'Oh, gee, double starred,' I echoed sarcastically. 'Great.' I paused. '*Why?*' I demanded.

He shook his head sadly. 'I can't tell you that, either.'

That did it. All the pent up anger exploded out at him. 'Well, why the hell are you here? And what the hell *can* you tell me?'

'Well . . .' he thought about it for a moment, my anger passing as easily off him as my hand had through him. 'Basically, only what you already know. Sort of, anyway.'

'That doesn't make any sense!' I yelled. 'I don't know what I know!'

'Shhh, Sam, please,' he said, pointing to his head. 'Have a little consideration.'

'Sorry,' I said sullenly. 'Well? What can you tell me?' I demanded again. 'There has to be something!'

He shrugged. 'That you're part of an experiment that went, shall we say, a little kaa-kaa.'

I couldn't believe what I was hearing. 'A little kaa-kaa,' I repeated. Very scientific, I thought. '*How* little kaa-kaa?' I asked suspiciously.

'Well . . .' he shrugged again. 'You're here.' Then he brightened. 'And let's not downplay that, Sam, that's a biggie. A first.'

'A first . . .'

He nodded. 'We're talking Nobel Prize time here. You should be very proud.'

I thought about it. 'Time travel,' I said, finally. 'Wow.' I was impressed, despite myself. But he was leaving something out, I realized. The kaa-kaa part. 'So what's the problem here?' I asked.

'Ah . . .' he smiled weakly, 'well, the thing is, we seem to be experiencing some technical difficulties in retrieving you.'

I stared at him for a moment, then began to tie another fly, just to keep myself occupied. 'That's great, Al,' I said sarcastically, 'I wake up in 1956 with a memory like Swiss cheese, and you tell me you're experiencing technical difficulties.' The line snapped in my hand. 'So, even if I *get* the Nobel Prize for whatever this experiment is, I probably won't be able to trip on over to Stockholm and accept it in person, will I?'

'Ah . . .' he said.

'But that's okay, Al,' I assured him with a sneer, 'you can always just accept it for me – we already know you look good in a tux.'

'Oh, Jesus, Sam, don't make this any worse than it already is,' he said with a sigh.

I didn't see how that was possible. 'Whose brainchild is this, anyway?' I demanded. 'Is it yours?'

He seemed to find some sort of secret humor in that question, and he bit back a smile. 'No,' he assured me, 'it's not mine.' Then he checked his watch and changed the subject – something he seemed expert at doing. 'We don't have much time,' he announced. 'What I started to tell you before is that Ziggy has computed five scenarios that might explain why we couldn't retrieve you this morning.'

'You tried?' I said, surprised. I remembered the vivid, surreal dream with the clouds and the earth dropping away, and wondered if that could have been someone trying to get me back.

'Of course we tried,' said Al. 'You wouldn't leap.'

'Oh, so now you're saying this is all my fault?' I said defensively.

Al shrugged. 'Possibly.' He wrinkled his forehead in thought. 'You didn't happen to tell anyone that you weren't really Tom Stratton, did you?'

I thought of my aborted conversation in the car with Peggy last night. Even my joking around with Bird Dog. 'Ah . . . sort of,' I admitted. 'But not *really*. Why?'

'Oh, Jesus, Sam!' Al exclaimed, 'retrieving you was dependent upon everyone believing that you *are* the person you replaced!'

'Well, how the hell was I supposed to remember that?' I sniped back. 'I don't remember *anything*! Besides,' I added, 'they didn't believe me.' I smiled ruefully. 'I mean, why would they? I look in the mirror and *I* don't believe me!'

Albert nodded and jotted something down on the paper. 'That's good – that's to be expected. To us, Tom Stratton looks just like you.'

'Oh,' I said, surprised. 'Then he's with you?'

'Of course,' Al said matter of factly. 'How do you think we located you?'

I shrugged. 'How the hell would I know?'

'When you went in,' Al continued, 'he came out. If it's any consolation,' he added thoughtfully, 'his memory is as full of holes as yours is.'

'As a matter of fact,' I said, 'it's not much consolation at all.'

'Hey, I was just trying to make you feel better,' Al said.

'Who . . . where does he think he is?' I asked, curious despite myself.

'He thinks he crashed his jet, and he's got temporary amnesia.'

'Lucky him,' I said grimly.

Al looked seriously at me. 'Sam, listen to me – this is of paramount importance here. Everyone here *has* to believe that you're really Tom Stratton when we try again on Tuesday.'

'Tuesday?' I asked, panicked. 'Can't we try before Tuesday?'

Al shook his head. 'Ziggy says Tuesday,' he said. He looked at me curiously. 'Why? You think you can't fake it for that long?'

'There might be a little problem with that one, Al,' I said sincerely. 'You can fake some things some of the time . . . but it just so happens that I'm scheduled to fly the X-2.'

'So?' he said.

'On Monday.'

Al paused in mid-page scrutiny to look up at me, but his eyes were still barricaded behind dark glasses, and I couldn't read his expression at all.

'Oh . . .' he said slowly.

'Right,' I agreed. 'Oh.'

'Sam,' he said, 'have you ever thought about taking flying lessons?'

CHAPTER ELEVEN

I don't know exactly how it happened, but for the rest of that easygoing weekend, I somehow managed to fall into Tom Stratton's normal routine just as I had apparently fallen into his life and his body.

Mikey and I arrived back at the house later that Saturday afternoon with nearly a dozen large German trout which he had caught; I had managed to strike out completely. I cleaned the fish while Peg poured us some fresh lemonade. Then Peg casually mentioned the fact that she was really happy that Mikey had been so successful – it seemed we could use all that trout the next afternoon at the big barbeque we were having. I smiled and pretended that's what I had been thinking, too.

'I can't believe I didn't catch a single fish,' I said apologetically.

'You tried, Dad,' Mikey chimed in supportively.

'Oh, honey,' Peg said, putting an understanding hand on my arm, 'that's okay. I know you've got a lot on your mind.'

No kidding, I thought ruefully.

Just like any normal suburban family on a normal Saturday evening in the fifties, we spent an hour in the front yard; I raked leaves while Peg watched Mikey ride his battered little bike up and down the block. Later, we barbequed big, juicy T-bone steaks and ate them with heated up canned string beans and a salad made of Iceberg lettuce and pinkish tomatoes. For dessert, Peg had made a jello mold, the kind I hadn't seen since I was a kid – three different colors in bright layers, festively enhanced with sliced bananas, maraschino cherries and canned pineapple chunks suspended like little airplanes in the quivering technicolor achievement.

'This is wonderful, honey,' I assured her, valiantly swallowing a mouthful of the repellent dessert.

'Oh, Tom, you've finally begun to like it!' Peg looked delighted. 'Now I won't feel like I'm just making it for Mikey and me!'

Jeez, I could have gotten out of it.

Mikey chattered away about the fishing trip and the new bike he wanted, hinting that it wasn't too early to start thinking about Christmas presents, and the afternoon passed into evening in a very unremarkable way. Unremarkable, that is, as long as the two people who I shared it with didn't somehow tumble to the fact that I wasn't really good old Tom Stratton. Other than that minor little oddity, the entire scene was like something from 'Ozzie and Harriet'. I had to stop myself from suggesting that if the new baby was a boy, we should name him Ricky and buy him a guitar.

After dinner, we all gathered around the Motorola and watched 'Beat the Clock' and 'People are Funny' – a great favorite of Mikey's, I discovered; he seemed to feel he and Art Linkletter were true kindred spirits. He especially liked the penalty phase of the show which, tonight, featured pie throwing. After that, we put Mikey to bed, and played a few hands of gin rummy at the kitchen table, until Peg yawned and said she absolutely had to go to bed. I told her I was restless, was going to stay up a little longer. She nodded sympathetically and toddled away to sleep.

It hadn't been a difficult night, I reflected, settling in front of the television again, not really. If I was a little on the quiet side, Peg had given me the perfect out by

understandingly chalking my silence up to being en-
grossed in my upcoming test flight. As a matter of fact,
it was all so simple and calm and friendly that I almost
felt guilty for wanting to get the hell out as soon as
possible. That was crazy, I reminded myself, as I tuned
in to the fifties version of late night television: 'Gun-
smoke' and 'Your Hit Parade.' There wasn't even any
eleven o'clock news to watch; the screen simply showed
the waving flag and some snow, and that was it.

I didn't try to call my father again; I figured my
memory would take me no further about who I really
was this evening than it had the last. And I couldn't let
myself get depressed about it, either. I had a far more
immediate issue to worry about, like how on earth I was
going to fake flying an experimental rocket three days
from now; even pretending to be Tom Stratton seemed
simple compared to that. But no easy solution presented
itself, and I mentally waved off Al's not so funny
suggestion that I 'learn how to fly.' In three days? Right.

The next afternoon, all the flyers and their families
descended on our back yard for a neighborly couple of
hours of grilling, beers, gossip, herding the kids, throwing a softball. Like that – simple domestic pleasures and
camaraderie. I found myself, an outsider pretending to
be an insider, watching the scene with a detached,
objective eye; I was surprised to find myself thinking that
maybe things really *had* been simpler back then – an idea,
I had a feeling, I would normally be very cynical about.
But it all seemed so . . . peaceful. Safe.

Two little girls were swinging on Mikey's set while I
patiently coached Mikey on the finer points of throwing
a curve ball. The sky above us was a canopy of bright,
clear blue, dotted with scattered puffs of white clouds.
Over at the barbeque, Bird Dog was teaching Jeannie
how to grill trout perfectly – he seemed by today to have

appropriated the blonde visitor for himself, and they were whispering in an intimate sort of way – about trout? I wondered.

Lucy, Sally and Peg were in the kitchen preparing the rest of the meal, and giggling about something – as I passed in and out for another beer, I heard a scrap of conversation that had something to do with 'doing it with his goggles on,' but they promptly shut up when they saw me.

Hah! I thought, so women had always talked about sex – it wasn't just the product of the sexual revolution. Oh boy, sexual revolution – there was a phrase from the future! I bit back a grin. I came back outside, passing by Doug and Tim – Lucy's husband – talking flying at the picnic table. Doug was using his hands to demonstrate some particular point.

'. . . then the nose snapped right and she did a half-roll and tucked into an inverted spin. I came off the power and neutralized the controls, but it didn't do diddly squat. If anything, the damned spin got flatter.'

I was fascinated by what they were saying, despite the fact that I really didn't understand any of it. I wondered suddenly if what these men were doing in 1956 – breaking speed records and sound barriers – was the precursor of whatever I was doing in – well, thirty or forty years later. 'Leaping,' as Al had called it.

Lucy came out with the paper plates and bumped her hip sexily against Doug's shoulder.

'Hi, babe,' he said, patting her on the rear end. Then he went right back to the topic at hand, saying to Tim, 'I didn't want to punchout inverted, but what the hell else could I do? I was down to five thousand and unwinding like a Green Stamp clock.'

I saw Lucy shoot him an exasperated look, and bit back another grin: so the men had always yammered about work while the women talked about sex.

Suddenly, there was a rush of air, followed by a whistling roar which grew louder and louder. Everyone looked up at the sky.

An F-86 Saber jet, so close it looked as if you could touch it, swept up just past the trees that lined the yard, executed a snappy roll, and then pulled abruptly up into a climb that looked absolutely vertical. I glanced over at Bird Dog, saw his grin of appreciation . . . and Jeannie's blanched face. She had her ears covered with her hands – she wasn't used to it. She wasn't a pilot's wife. Not yet, anyway.

Peg and Sally, recognizing the sounds, had rushed from the house and stood just outside the kitchen door, shading their eyes to watch the rest of the show. The jet reached the peak of its climb, then suddenly appeared to completely stall out. It nosed down and began a plummet straight back towards earth at a stomach-turning angle. I heard Jeannie's gasp even over the noise of the jet. Then, just as it seemed as if it would certainly crash, the F-86 pulled out of the fall, turned in a fast half-roll, and thundered past us upside down. There was a smattering of applause and catcalls from the pilots in the yard.

'And all that was done just to impress you, Sweet Pea,' Bird Dog informed Jeannie, whose eyes were as big as saucers.

'Me?' she asked, puzzled.

Bird Dog grinned. 'That was Tony,' he said.

'Oh,' Jeannie said, shading her eyes.

In the distance, we could see the F-86's landing gear drop, and Tony bring the jet down towards the runway at the base.

Bird Dog reached into his jean pocket and flipped his keys to Jeannie. 'Go on and get him, honey. Tell him we've got fresh trout on the grill.'

Jeannie smiled in surprise. 'Okay,' she replied and jogged towards the T-Bird.

I felt Mikey standing beside me, and looked down at him. On his face was a mixture of awe and desire. 'Wow!' he exclaimed. 'Did you see that snap roll? And that flip he did at the top?'

I nodded. 'Sure did,' I said.

'What do you call that, Dad?'

'Got me,' I shrugged, forgetting to be Tom Stratton for the moment.

'A hammerhead stall,' Bird Dog said, with a curious look at me.

I remembered what Al had said about the importance of being believed, and I grinned at Bird Dog. 'Just practicing,' I said.

'Wow!' said Mikey again. 'That's really something, I want to do that someday!' He looked up at me. 'You ever do a hammerhead stall, Dad?'

'Oh,' I shrugged dismissively, 'nothing to it, I can do them in my sleep,' I assured him with a straight face.

'Someday I'm gonna be able to do that,' Mikey exclaimed, 'just like you . . .'

Then I noticed that Peg was watching this exchange intently. She was sort of leaning against the doorjamb, and her face looked a little tense and flushed. She caught me looking at her, and turned and hurried back into the kitchen.

'I'm going to go help your Mom in the kitchen,' I said to Mikey.

'Aw, Dad,' Mikey replied, disappointed. 'What about the Little League tryouts?'

I tossed the softball to Bird Dog, who caught it deftly. 'Here,' I said, 'practice Mikey's curve ball with him, would you?'

Bird Dog threw an understanding glance in the

direction of the kitchen. 'Sure, Pard,' he replied. 'Come on, lil' Pard,' he said to Mikey, striding off towards the large open area beyond the barbeque, 'let's you and me show your dad what a real curve ball looks like!'

Inside the cheerful little kitchen, bright sunlight streamed through the colorful curtains, bathing everything in the room with a warm glow. As I came in from the backyard, Peg was standing by the sink, pouring herself a glass of tap water.

I walked casually to the refrigerator and grabbed a bottle of beer. I pried the top off with a wall mounted Coca Cola opener, and took a long swallow. It felt cool and good going down.

'Peg?' I said.

'Hmm?' She had moved over to the kitchen table and was suddenly very busy chopping cucumbers, adding them to a brimming salad bowl full of greens.

'Are you okay?'

She turned and smiled at me, but I could tell it was an effort. 'Of course,' she said.

'You look a little ... shaky or something,' I said tentatively.

'No, really, I'm fine,' Peg insisted. 'It's just this heat – you know how I am, I swear, I'll just never get used to it.'

'Peg,' I said seriously, 'it's the flight, isn't it? That's what's worrying you?'

She shook her head negatively. 'No,' she said. 'Of course it's not. Well,' she amended her statement, looking up at me with clear, honest eyes, 'no more than usual, anyway.'

'I'm sorry,' I said spontaneously. 'I don't want to put you through that.'

'Come on, Tom,' she said, a smile on her face. 'I knew what I was getting into when I married you, so there's no sense in being a baby about it. We – ' she gestured outside to include the wives '– all feel the same way. We just live with it.' She looked quizzically at me. 'But I never used to think you noticed.'

'Oh,' I shrugged, 'well . . .' So much for latter day male sensitivity.

'But thanks for noticing,' Peg said softly.

I was embarrassed, at a loss for words. I glanced around the kitchen, and my eyes came back to rest at the table where Peg was working. 'Hey,' I said impulsively, 'want me to help? I make a mean Caesar salad.'

Peg wrinkled her brow.

'Just kidding,' I added hastily.

'I know,' she said drily, 'you can't even boil an egg for yourself.'

'But seriously,' I said, 'I meant it about the way you look.'

Peg laughed and patted her stomach. 'That's your fault, mister.'

'Peg,' I said, 'that's not what I mean, and you know it.'

Peg nodded. 'Yes,' she agreed, 'I know it. But I really am all right. And there's no sense in dwelling on things you can't change.'

'You're right,' I said. Hah! I thought.

'Come on, Tom, you're just in the way in the kitchen! Go back out there and have another beer and spend some more time with Mikey.'

'You sure?' I hovered in the doorway.

'I'm sure,' Peg smiled. 'He's thrilled. You haven't spent this much time with him since he got hit by the bus.'

Jesus! Mikey had been hit by a bus? I had to stop myself from reacting with surprise and horror.

'Well . . . okay,' I said, and turned towards the door.

'Hey . . . flyboy!' Peg's voice was full of mischief.

I turned back. Peg had moved up beside me. I was completely unprepared for what happened next.

'This is for being such a thoughtful husband,' she said. Then she put her arms around me and kissed me – not a chaste peck on the cheek, but a full, soft, sexy kiss. The kind of kiss that was meant to remind me . . . And I was schmuck enough to respond wholeheartedly.

When we parted lips, we just stood there, staring at each other. I could tell that Peg was a little confused by the kiss. As far as I was concerned, it had been a more than satisfactory kiss; but of course, it wasn't the kiss she was used to.

'Hey, you two lovebirds, come on outside and join the rest of us – food's ready!' It was Bird Dog's voice, and I was suddenly thankful for the interruption.

I backed away from Peg guiltily. 'Got to eat trout while it's sizzling,' I said.

'That's not the only thing that's sizzling around here, mister!' Peg winked at me, then turned back to the table. 'Here,' she said, 'you take the salad. I'll get the rolls and butter.'

I grabbed the big wooden salad bowl gratefully and backed hastily out the door. Outside in the yard, I took a deep breath, and walked calmly to the picnic table with its gaily checked red and white paper cloth.

Jesus, I thought, things could get out of hand. I would really have to be careful. No, that wasn't it at all. I would really have to get out of here – *that* was it!

'Tom!' It was Peg, calling to me from the doorway. 'Dr Ernst is on the phone . . . he says you have to come to the base right away.'

CHAPTER TWELVE

Here's an observation: bureaucracy transcends all time limitations. I had rushed through the barbeque and left Peg with the task of cleaning up in order to get to the base right away, only to discover when I arrived that Dr Ernst and Dr Burger had been called away for some unspecified emergency.

Great, I thought, now what do I do? Sit here and feel sorry for myself? Feel guilty for kissing Peg? Well, hell, I thought suddenly, might as well take advantage of being unobserved to check out the X-2. I strolled casually into the hangar, the sunset at my back, feeling like the hero of some movie.

It stood there gleaming in the sun's rays, powerful, frightening. It really was a beautiful machine. I walked slowly around it, sliding my hand along the sharp needle nose; just imagining what it must be like in the cockpit of this sleekly crafted rocket gave me goose bumps. For the moment, I could just enjoy imagining being in it, and put off thinking that the fantasy might really come to pass – and turn into a living nightmare.

I peered through the clear plexiglass bubble that covered the cockpit, and stared at a bewildering array of panels, instruments, switches and controls. There were no printed instructions here. It was a sudden infusion of reality.

'Pretty simple, isn't it?'

I jumped, then looked up and saw Al grinning at me from across the cockpit.

'Jesus!' I exclaimed, 'can't you just . . . fade in or something?'

He looked considerably less hung over than he had the last time I saw him; of course, I had no idea how time where he came from related to time where I was.

Al's grin broadened. 'Sure,' he said. 'You just tell me how to fade in agitated carbon quarks, and I'll be the one who gets the Nobel Prize.'

'Okay, okay,' I said irritably, 'just don't sneak up on me. My nerves are shot as it is.'

'Hey,' protested Al, 'you're not the only one, buddy. You know, this isn't easy on me, either. I happen to be giving up an entire weekend with a very amenable redhead, if you get my drift.'

I shook my head in disbelief. 'I'm stuck in a time warp and all you can talk about is women.'

Al shrugged. 'They happen to be extremely important to me,' he said as he studied the inside of the cockpit again. 'You know,' he said after a moment, 'Ziggy spit out a new theory.'

I perked up immediately. 'A new theory . . . to get me back?'

Al nodded. 'Uh huh,' he said. 'Actually, it's more of a, well, a *philosophy* than a theory.'

'Philosophy?' I echoed doubtfully.

'Yeah.' Al's eyebrow quirked up cynically. 'But if you ask me, personally, I think it's complete bullshit.'

'Oh,' I deflated.

'Even if Ziggy *is* predicting a seventy-seven per cent chance of success.'

'Seventy-seven?' I felt my flagging spirits begin to rise. 'That's pretty high.'

Al flip-flopped his hand. 'He said we had a ninety-six per cent chance of retrieving you this morning.'

I looked at him and sighed. 'I really didn't need to

hear that, Al, or whoever the hell you really are.'

He stared at me, his brow creased in a little frown. 'You still don't remember me?'

I shook my head no.

'Or the project?'

No again.

'Christ,' he sighed, making me feel like a retarded student. He walked through the plane to me. Right through it, as if it didn't exist. I shook my head to clear it, although by this time, I should have expected the bizarre to happen whenever Al appeared.

'You know,' said Al, now standing beside me, 'it's bad enough that I have to give Dick and Jane explanations to the President, but being reduced to giving one to you . . .' he shook his head sadly. 'Pitiful.'

'The President . . . you mean, of the United States?' I ventured.

'Well, of course,' said Al. He looked at me with a new, hopeful glint in his eye. 'Do you know who that is?' he asked.

I thought about it for a moment, then shrugged. 'Nope,' I admitted, 'but it's probably not Eisenhower, right?'

Al snorted in disgust. 'Right,' he said. He pulled a string from his pocket and began to fiddle with it, stretching it into a taut line in front of my face. 'Okay, Sam,' he said. 'Listen carefully and see if any of this rings a bell with you. One end of this string is your birth. The other is your death. You with me so far?'

I nodded.

'Okay,' he continued, 'mark off each day of your life on the string, tie the ends together.' He proceeded to do so. 'Now you have a loop. Ball the loop . . .' he crunched up the knotted string in his hand, '. . . and random dates touch each other out of sequence. So April fifth in seventy-four might be touching August fifteenth in fifty-six and January eighth in eighty-one . . . you get the idea?'

I nodded again.

'Now,' he said, 'leaping from one point on the string to another . . .'

'. . . would move you backward or forward within your own lifetime.' I finished the sentence for him, the light finally beginning to dawn.

'That's correct,' said Al.

'But . . .' I said, '. . . *how*?'

He looked at me with penetrating dark eyes. 'Sam,' he said softly, 'does the term "Quantum Leap" maybe set off a little ding-dong noise anywhere in whatever is left of your brain?'

'Oh my God!' I said, memory flooding back in an unexpected surge. The words came out in a machine-gun staccato. 'The disappearance of a sub-atomic particle from one location and its simultaneous appearance at another!' I looked at him for confirmation, and he nodded. 'But only sub-atomic particles can quantum leap . . . and they do it in linear time!' I finished triumphantly.

'Until our project,' Al interjected.

And just as suddenly as my memory had reappeared, it was gone again: I drew a complete blank. 'I can't remember!' I wailed. 'God damn it!'

I pounded the X-2 in frustration and stalked away. Al followed, taking a short-cut through the wing.

'I asked you to stop doing that!' I snapped at him.

'What?' He stopped smack in the middle, super-imposed in a ghostlike image.

'Walking through things!'

'You want me to walk around what's not there?' Al shrugged. 'Okay.'

As if he were humoring a spoiled child on the verge of throwing a tantrum, he made a big, dramatic show out of walking out of the wing, then all the way around it – giving it wide berth. He joined up with me at the tail and took a little bow.

'Better?' he said snidely.

I held up my hand in a placating gesture. 'I'm sorry. It's just that I can't remember – I think I do, and then I come up against these walls, and it's driving me crazy.' I sighed. 'So what about this latest theory Ziggy has to get me back?'

'Well,' Al said, 'like I told you, it's off the wall, as far as I'm concerned. I mean, you've got to believe that there's more to all this than a mere quantum leap back to fifty-six.'

'A *mere* quantum leap?' I echoed sarcastically.

'Hey,' Al protested, 'those are Ziggy's words, not mine. He's a gauge computer, and you know how they love putting us down.' Off my blank look, he added, 'Well, you used to know, anyway.'

'Just go on,' I said.

'Okay. Ziggy's theory is that Time – with a capital T – or God, or something like that was waiting for your quantum leap. Well, anybody's quantum leap, I guess. To correct a mistake.'

'What?' Now I was really confused. 'What *kind* of mistake?'

'I don't know,' Al shrugged. 'Something that happened in the past, I guess. To be more specific, in this particular case, something that happened to Captain Tom Stratton, since he's the one you replaced.'

I thought about it for a moment, but it still didn't make sense. 'I don't get it,' I said.

'Me neither, not really. It's like . . .' Al thought for a moment, 'like once that wrong is put right, then you'll just snap right back like a pimp's suspenders. My words,' he added, 'not Ziggy's.'

'Okay,' I said, 'saying I buy this crackbrained theory

– and I'm not saying I do buy it, not at all. But saying I do, can we get just a little more specific here? Once *what's* put right?'

Al seemed to hesitate. 'Captain Tom Stratton was . . . killed.'

I felt a sense of foreboding, a sense of inevitability. 'Go on,' I said.

'He was killed,' Al went on grimly, 'trying to break Mach-three in the X-2.'

'Like I'm scheduled to try to do Monday,' I whispered.

Al nodded. 'Yeah. But if Ziggy's right,' he said optimistically, 'all you have to do is break Mach-three and live!'

I stared at him as if he were a raving lunatic, then turned on my heel and stalked angrily out of the hangar. As I emerged into the late sunlight, and hurried furiously toward the flight line, Al was at my heels, practically running to keep up with me.

'Sam . . .' he said.

'No way! No!' I kept going.

'Hey, pal,' Ziggy panted, 'it's not my theory – don't kill the messenger.'

'There has *got* to be another way,' I insisted.

'Hah!' Al stared at me while trying to keep up the pace. 'The *next* one only has a fifty-two per cent chance of working!'

Anything had to be better than going up in that plane. 'I'll take it,' I said firmly.

'Be my guest,' Al shrugged. 'It only requires you to be at ground zero during an atomic detonation.'

'*What?!*'

'In the micro-second before you disintegrate . . . you leap back.'

I stopped abruptly, kicking up a cloud of fine dry dust, and stared with furious intensity at him.

'You asked,' Al said defensively.

'Give me that . . .' I grabbed for his clipboard and the list of possibilities. Of course, my hand passed right through it. 'God damn it,' I muttered.

'Sam . . .'

'Never mind,' I said, irritated. 'Just tell me what else you've got to offer.'

Al looked a little offended. 'This isn't a shopping list, you know – the possibilities are extremely limited.' He consulted the list and shook his head. 'The odds drop into the low teens after that one. Let's see . . .' he read from the list, 'it looks as if your best shot is freezing the brain until all electricity has ceased.'

'Pardon me, but I believe that's called death,' I said through clenched teeth.

'I didn't say it would be *easy*,' he replied.

I threw my hands up in frustration and began to stride across the tarmac again, just to work off some negative energy. Al chased after me.

'Hey, hey! Slow down, would you? I'm still fighting a hangover!'

I just picked up the pace. Al always seemed to be fighting a hangover. Maybe this would teach him. Or shake his brain loose and make him come up with a way to get me out of this predicament.

He raced along beside me, grimacing with every step. 'Okay,' he said, 'okay! You want a sure thing? I got one for you.'

I slowed my pace down, but not enough to make his jogging much easier. 'You do?' I asked suspiciously. 'What?'

'Just don't,' he said, gasping, 'do anything at all.'

'Huh?'

'No experiments, no risks involved. No . . . leaping. Just live.'

I thought about what he was suggesting. Maybe he had a point, maybe it was a possibility. But what kind of life would it be? Okay, it might be a choice, but it posed a whole new set of problems.

Taking my silence for interest, Al continued. 'Look at it this way, Sam. Barring accidental death or some hideous fatal disease they haven't found the cure for yet – here – you'll be back in forty years.' He stared quizzically at me. 'It's the safest plan.'

But was it the smartest plan? How do you weigh the option of physical safety against living your life as a total lie. And involving everyone else around you in it. I had no idea, and in that instant, no answers presented themselves. It was a question for a philosopher, and whatever I was in my real, future life, I was pretty sure I wasn't that.

And not just that, but what about my leaping counterpart – the one who hadn't seemed to have had a choice in any of this. What kind of life would I be sending him into? Even if I decided I had the right to make that kind of decision for myself . . . 'What about Tom Stratton?' I asked.

Al nodded. 'Tom, yeah.' He thought about it for a moment. 'I guess he'll live forward from where he is now.' He paused to consider something, then chuckled. 'Technically, you know, he could very well wind up being the oldest man alive.'

'Bully for him,' I said glumly, 'then he could have his birthday announced by Willard Scott. I'm sure that will make up for it all.'

'You remember Willard Scott?' Al asked, horrified, 'and you don't remember *me*?'

I brushed the question aside. It wasn't the time for jokes, and besides, even though the name had popped out of my mouth, I didn't really remember anyone with that name. 'And what about Peg?' I demanded. 'And Mikey?'

'What about them?' Al seemed a little puzzled by the question.

'I don't know,' I said uncomfortably, 'it's just . . . I don't want to hurt them, but there's no way I could live out a lifetime pretending to be Tom Stratton – even if I couldn't tell them the truth, I guess I'd just have to leave or something.' Even the *idea* of Peg and Mikey deserted with no explanation made me feel queasy. Sad, guilty. Guilty. 'I don't think I could . . .'

'They were going to lose him on Monday anyway,' Al reminded me.

'But *they* don't know that,' I said.

'No,' he agreed with a sigh, 'they don't.'

It was all too much of a mind-wearying puzzle for me. I just couldn't untangle it, not so quickly, so I went back to the most immediate issue. 'And speaking of Monday . . .' I said to Al.

'Well, that's the thing,' said Al happily, 'you don't really have to worry about any of this, not if you bust Mach three and survive. Because if you do that, then they could have him – the real Tom Stratton – hanging around in his own life for the next forty or fifty years.'

'That's what I call looking on the bright side of things, Al,' I said sarcastically, 'except for one itty bitty little fact that you seem to have conveniently forgotten. I can't fly!'

'You don't need to,' he assured me. 'I'll be along – I'll be your co-pilot.'

'Oh, for Christ's sake, Al!' I exploded, 'You're a *hologram*!'

He smiled. 'I'm also an ex-astronaut.'

I digested the information in bemused silence. '*Really?*' I said finally.

'You know,' Al said, ignoring the inference, 'the hardest part of flying is taking off and landing. In this instance, however, the mother ship does the first one for you.'

'That's true,' I said thoughtfully, trying to envision it.

'Once you're dropped from the belly, all you have to do is fire the rockets – no big deal – and then just apply a little back pressure to the stick.' He seemed to be planning it out in his mind as he went along.

'Oh, is that all?' I enquired mildly. 'It sounds like Latin to me.'

'You were good in Latin,' he said casually, then caught himself. 'Oops. Scratch that. No, really, that isn't hard. You'll shoot up to forty thousand. You put a little forward pressure on the stick, and whoosh! You're on your merry way to Mach-three.' He nodded in satisfaction. 'I like it.'

I didn't. 'You forgot something, Al,' I reminded him in a sing-song voice.

Al wrinkled his brow in thought. 'Oh,' he said, 'landing.'

'Very good,' I said.

'Landing,' he repeated, a frown creasing his brow. 'The thing is, you could never land the X-2, not even with me helping.'

'So I'm dead,' I concluded.

'No, no, no!' Al insisted. 'You couldn't do it, so you *don't* do it.'

Suddenly I caught on to what he was saying. 'I get it,' I exclaimed. 'I don't land, I eject.'

'Bingo,' Al said with a small smile. 'You bail out, and the X-2 does a spectacular crash and burn, while you float back to earth on a bubble of silk.'

'You're getting poetic, Al,' I said.

He ignored the dig, racing ahead with his plans. 'The

minute you touch down, Tom leaps back. You leap forward. And I,' he finished with a triumphant glint in his eye, 'head for Vegas with the redhead.'

I thought about it all. If what Al had been telling me – the little he had been telling me – about quantum leaping was true, perhaps there was a chance, after all.

'It might work,' I said cautiously. Maybe I could really bust this joint, get back to – wherever. Get my memory, my life, back.

'Of course it will work,' Al said, offended.

'A minute ago you said it was all bullshit,' I reminded him.

Al shrugged. 'That was before I thought it out.'

CHAPTER THIRTEEN

I stood there on the warm tarmac thinking about what Al had just proposed. The rays of the late day sun slanted over the base, glowing, eerie and surreal, highlighting the encapsulated feeling of the place: just pale desert, a paler dry lakebed, distant mauve mountains and deep blue sky surrounded us. It was all so removed from the real world, so much – with what went on here – a world unto itself. I realized I actually liked it, in a strange sort of way: it made all things seem possible. I wondered if it was this feeling that infused test pilots with the guts to do what they did.

'I wonder,' I mused aloud, 'I just wonder if we might pull this off.'

Al shrugged. '*I* think we can,' he said, 'but in the final analysis, it's up to you.'

'The choice, you mean,' I said, 'the choice whether or not I climb into that thing tomorrow.'

Al nodded. 'But let me remind you, Sam, you're gonna have a hell of a time trying to weasel out of flying tomorrow. No one's going to understand. So if you decide not to try our little plan, you'd better come up with a damned good excuse why you can't fly.'

Just as he finished his dire prediction, I saw a convoy, two jeeps and a couple of flat-bed trucks, heading in my direction. As they passed by, Weird Ernie pulled to a stop in one of them. 'Sorry, Tom,' he said, 'a little problem kicking up with the winds and the equipment that was left at the lake bed.' He jerked his thumb over his shoulder towards one of the trucks. I could see that it held the wreckage of a crashed X-2. 'We had to retrieve that stuff.'

I nodded understandingly, feeling my stomach flip-flop at the sight of all that jumbled metal.

'Hop in,' he motioned me.

'Okay.'

'See you later, Sam,' I heard Al say as I settled into the jeep. I looked around, but he was gone.

After Weird Ernie had directed the technicians where to put the pieces of the rocket, Weird Ernie, Dr Burger and I settled ourselves down in the same office off the hangar where all the pilots had gathered on Friday. 'What's up?' I asked.

'Sorry to pull you away from the barbeque,' Weird Ernie said, 'but after hearing what you men were saying on Friday, Dr Burger and I felt it was imperative that we get going on this memory test for all of you, that we not waste any time.'

Dr Burger nodded in agreement.

'We've been working on it for the past two days solid,' Weird Ernie went on, 'and we decided this morning that it was in complete enough shape to use. Now we just need you to fill out the questionnaire before you take the X-2 up tomorrow . . .'

That sent a shiver up my spine, but I nodded genially. 'Sure,' I said, 'tell me about it.'

'Well,' Dr Burger said, clearing his throat, 'Dr Ernst and I devised this test in order to evaluate Captain Birdell's theory that coming increasingly closer to Mach-three has some sort of proportionate inverse negative effect on the memory.'

I sucked in my cheeks to keep from laughing – all that scientific jargon wrapped around a joke of Bird Dog's – and nodded gravely. 'Uh-huh . . .'

Dr Burger fixed me with a very suspicious look. I had the feeling that he was just a little less gullible than Weird Ernie, and his next words confirmed my suspicion. 'Quite frankly, Tom, if the claim had come only from you, we would have been . . . skeptical. To say the least.'

'We all know your penchant for practical jokes,' Weird Ernie added.

This time, I couldn't refrain from grinning. 'Doctor,' I assured him, 'trust me on this. Any memory losses I suffer won't be faked!' Well, it was nothing but the truth, wasn't it?

'Hmmm, well . . . yes. That's good,' Dr Burger said reluctantly.

'You know, Captain,' Weird Ernie continued, 'we may just be on the verge of something here, something *much* more far reaching, greater in its implications, than merely breaking Mach-three.' He stared at me intensely. 'Do you understand?'

Personally, it was a little hard for me to see: at the moment, there wasn't anything I could think of that was more far reaching than breaking Mach-three. Because if I didn't break it, I would be dead. Or something. But I nodded as if I agreed.

'I guess,' I said, 'I mean, I'm not exactly sure *what* it would prove, but I can certainly see that it would be important.'

Dr Burger tamped down on the unlit pipe he was holding, then held a match to it. He puffed a few times to get it going, and a rich, fruity smell drifted through the hangar office. 'It would be more than important,' he said solemnly. 'It would be monumental.' Then he reached across the desk and pulled out a stapled stack of papers from their resting place beside a manual Royal typewriter, that old black upright model – it looked positively archaic to me.

Weird Ernie pointed at the papers. 'That's it,' he said solemnly. 'The questionnaire. It has two hundred questions . . .'

'Two hundred and seven,' Dr Burger corrected him.

'. . . to benchmark your memory as it is right now,' Weird Ernie continued as if the interruption hadn't happened. 'We're calling it the Ernst-Burger Engramic Standard . . .'

Dr Burger blew a puff of aromatic smoke into the air. 'I thought we were calling it the Burger-Ernst Engramic Standard,' he said mildly.

I bit back a smile – watching these two guys bicker was like watching a dual stand-up comedy routine, Laurel and Hardy or something.

Dr Burger surveyed the pages he held. 'We've tried to compile questions that would give us an accurate and definitive cross-section of your memory . . .'

Good luck, I thought.

'Some of them are completely standard, of course, like the current date, place of birth, your mother's maiden name . . .'

Not so standard as you think, Doc, I thought, recalling Al's snipe about my not even knowing who the president was. Oh boy.

'. . . you know,' he continued, 'the usual kinds of rote statistics. But most,' he gave me a cautionary look, 'most will only *appear* to be insignificant.' He paused and flipped through the pages, picking out questions at random. 'Such as, what was the coldest you've ever been? Who was your second best friend in college?'

He handed me the questionnaire. 'Where did you first make love?'

I grinned as I took the pages from him. 'At least you didn't ask, to who?'

Dr Burger raised an eyebrow. 'Actually, Dr Ernst

suggested we ask that,' he said disdainfully, 'but we decided that "where" is more meaningful – in terms of this test.'

'And more discreet,' said Weird Ernie.

'Oh, definitely,' I agreed. 'Definitely more discreet.' I flipped casually through the pages. 'Interesting,' I said. 'It's sort of like a personal "Trivial Pursuit".'

There was a moment of blank silence in the office, and I realized my gaffe.

Luckily, no one else did. 'That's not a bad name,' Dr Burger said thoughtfully, 'not bad at all. The Burger-Ernst Engramic Trivial Pursuit.'

'Ernst-Burger,' said Weird Ernie. He looked at me. 'We need to have this completely filled out before you take off tomorrow – I thought you would need this evening to do it. After you land, we'll have you fill it out again.'

After I land, I thought. If I land. If . . . who lands? 'Okay,' I said.

'If there are any significant changes in your memory, we should be able to detect them easily.'

You bet, I thought, smiling as I looked over the questions.

'Any questions, Captain?'

Not any you can answer, I thought. 'Ah . . . no, not really,' I said. 'It seems simple enough.'

'You can reach either of us at home if there's anything on there that puzzles you,' Dr Burger added. 'Don't hesitate to call – this needs to be done just right in order to work.'

I shook my head. 'I think I can figure it out,' I said, tongue planted firmly in cheek. 'I'll have it for you first thing tomorrow morning.'

I rolled the pages up into a narrow tube of paper, and saluted the good doctors with it. 'Doctors,' I said genially.

I walked out into the hangar and took another look at the X-2 – the thing that would prove to be my salvation. Or destruction. Would I do it? Would I fly, risking it all? Behind me, Weird Ernie and Dr Burger's voices drifted out from the office.

'Doctor,' I heard Weird Ernie say with a tamped down excitement in his voice, 'this could be amazing. We could be on the brink of a momentous discovery.'

I heard Dr Burger chuckle. 'We could also be on the brink of being the butt of a momentous joke,' he said.

Momentous certainly seemed to be a favorite vocabulary word around here. If only you knew, I thought, and strolled out of the hangar toward the gleaming Chevy. If only you knew.

*　　*　　*

Later that evening, after we had cleaned up the remnants of the barbeque and Mikey and Peg had gone to bed, I settled into a comfortable armchair and took a look at the questionnaire I was supposed to fill out for the good doctors.

There wasn't any way of getting out of it, and there certainly wasn't any way of learning enough about the real Tom Stratton in a mere couple of hours to come anywhere near hitting the real thing in answering the questions. Earlier, I had toyed briefly with the idea of making a game of it, of having Peg help me so I could fake it. But I didn't really want to do that – the idea made me squeamish for Peg's sake, and besides, I just couldn't figure out a way to get her to answer certain questions without scaring the hell out of her again.

For instance, how could I get Tom Stratton's mother's maiden name? 'Peg,' I imagined myself saying. 'Can you believe this? They want to know mom's maiden name. Isn't that silly?' Then I'd pause. 'By the way, Peg, I actually seem to have *forgotten* mom's maiden name. Isn't *that* silly? What was it again?'

No, it would never wash. Well, what the hell, I thought, staring down at the pages. I would just go ahead and answer the questions like myself. Sam, that is. If I died in the crash of the X-2 the next day, I wouldn't have to deal with it: they would all chalk the answers on the questionnaire up to a wild practical joke. On the other hand, if I didn't die, I wouldn't have to deal with it, either. I would be back in my own time, and Tom Stratton would be back, stuck having to cope with explanations.

I thought about that for a moment, then came to the conclusion: so what? It was the least he could do, I figured; after all, if he came back, it would mean I had saved his life. Let *him* take some heat from the docs!

Of course, being Sam-the-blank, there were still questions I couldn't answer, anyway. Even about myself. Like – well, like what my mother's maiden name was. There *was* a certain amount of ironic humor to be found in all of this. So I put pencil to paper, and just barrelled on through, answering the things I could, with bits and pieces of a memory that seemed to spring up from someplace I couldn't reach into at will. And I actually had some fun with it.

Now, I thought, *here* was something intriguing: when it came to date of birth, I automatically wrote 'August 8, 1953.' Hmm, I thought, if that was my real birthdate, then somewhere out there, a three-year-old Sam was lurching around the barn. Interesting thought.

Question: 'What had the most positive impact on you in high school?' That was easy, I thought. 'Mini-skirts,' I wrote.

'What had the most negative impact on you in high

school?' I grinned in painful recollection. *That* was even easier. 'Pantyhose.'

I wondered what Weird Ernie and Dr Burger would make of those words – words I was almost certain were non-existent words in 1956.

'What do you do when you feel lonely?' That was a good one. I thought for a moment, then wrote, 'I rent a video and micro-wave some popcorn.' Hmm, did that mean I wasn't married? It certainly sounded that way. It also sounded as if I wasn't exactly a wild, partying kind of a guy.

'Where did you first make love?' 'In the back of a panel truck at a Grateful Dead concert,' I wrote. Wow! Good luck with that one, guys, I thought, and chuckled to myself.

I was really getting into it, now. I went to town with answers I knew they would never make sense of. I threw in pet rocks, waterbeds, streaking, war protests, disco, slam-dancing, word processing, moonwalking, and early pregnancy home testing kits. I left out AIDS, Charles Manson, Bangladesh, the Greenhouse effect, Buddy Holly's death and Richard Nixon's presidency – they could get the *really* bad pieces of news as they happened. Sort of on the 'need to know' principle.

After I had finished filling out the forms, I got up and stretched. I walked over to the living room window and gazed out at the peaceful street, houses neat and dark, everyone asleep, moon shining. Suddenly, I felt very sad. I wondered if it was sadness at the idea of leaving this odd little glitch in life. Of course, there was always the option of refusing to fly the next day, and just remaining where I was. Al had said it: it was the least risky thing to do. But I couldn't conjure up a single plausible reason to use to get out of the flight.

I walked over to the phone and just stood by it, tracing

the receiver with my fingers, stroking it lightly as if the touch of it, the igniting of a tactile sense, would spark the rest of my memory. I could almost picture my father, but I still couldn't remember my name, or our phone number.

But I *did* have an unexpected memory, and it *was* about Dad. I suddenly recalled, as if I were a small boy again, that I had always gone to him when an important decision had to be made. That I had always felt that I couldn't make that kind of decision without talking to him. And then he had died, and I didn't have that option anymore.

I knew this with a visceral, gut-wrenching sense of emotional truth, with pure clarity, as I stood there in the darkened room. And suddenly, I knew with equal clarity that he hadn't actually ever *made* any of those decisions for me. He had just listened to me work through the problems and watched as I had come to my own con-clusions. He had allowed me to find my own way, and in doing so, had been the best teacher I could have had. He had seen to it that I learned to make decisions for myself – which was precisely what I was doing right now.

It was the oddest way of having a recollection, because it wasn't really a recollection at all. There was nothing tangible about it. There was no specific problem I remembered going to him with; there was no memory of a crucial incident or life-and-death decision. There was just this feeling of . . . comprehension.

'Tom?'

I looked up from my reverie, and saw Peg standing in the doorway in her baby doll pajamas. She looked sleepy and touseled.

'You should be asleep,' I told her gently.

'So should you,' she replied softly.

We smiled at each other in the dim room, smiled with a mutual understanding of exactly what was keeping us both awake.

Peg padded into the kitchen and poured herself a glass of milk. She held up the bottle to show me, a silent question, and I shook my head no. Then she rinsed out the glass in the sink, staring fixedly out the kitchen window at the moonlit street, just the way I had, with a wistful look in her eye.

Then she crossed the room and came to stand beside me. She put a gentle hand on my chin. 'You're really worried about breaking the record, aren't you?' she asked.

I shook my head. 'No.'

She smiled up at me and shook her head as if she didn't believe me. 'You'll do it, Tom. You'll be the fastest man alive.'

She didn't know how much irony there was in that statement. Fast, hell, I apparently could cross time boundaries with a single leap.

Peg took my hand and led me over to the arm chair, then pushed me gently into it. She crawled onto my lap and cuddled up. 'Promise me something?' she asked.

'What?'

She looked at me with calm, serious eyes. 'Promise first,' she said.

'That's silly,' I smiled down at her. 'How can I possibly promise something if I don't even know what it is I'm promising?'

'Shh,' Peg said putting her fingers to my lips. 'Come on, just promise.'

I looked into those clear blue eyes and gave in. 'Okay,' I said, 'I promise.'

'Good,' Peg said contentedly.

'Well?' I asked her. 'Aren't you going to tell me?'

Peg smiled and put my hand on her abdomen. I could

feel the baby, restless and kicking, practicing to be a place kicker. Or a Rockette. Peg kissed me gently on the mouth. 'I'll tell you when you come home tomorrow. Deal?'

Oh, boy. 'Deal,' I assured her.

CHAPTER FOURTEEN

'Good morning, Captain Stratton.' Dr Burger smiled genially at me as I walked into the hangar office.

I felt like asking what was so good about it, but I contented myself with a simple hello instead.

'So, are you ready to become the fastest man on earth?'

'I guess I'm about as ready as I'll ever be,' I replied truthfully. I felt incredibly clunky and stupid, zipped and buckled into a silver pressure suit that looked exactly like something out of a fifties sci-fi movie. And there was a very good reason for that: I seemed to be *living* in one of those movies. I felt like I ought to be saying things like, 'My name is Zoron, and I come from Planet X to bring you greetings.'

Instead, I said, 'Well . . . here you go,' and handed the questionnaire across the desk to Dr Burger.

He riffled through the pages and nodded in satisfaction. 'What did you think of our little test?' he asked.

I was relieved that he hadn't noticed the blanks I'd had to leave right off, and I pretended to give the question some serious thought. 'Gee, Doc,' I said finally, 'it was kind of interesting, but I'm really not sure how useful it'll be to gauge a memory loss.'

'No?' he frowned.

I shrugged. 'Oh, well, who knows?' I said. Then I grinned at him. 'But filling it out last night sure brought back a lot of vivid old recollections alive again for me!'

'Oh . . .' He appeared to relax. 'Well, that's a start, anyway. When you report back here after the flight, I'm going to have you fill it out again immediately, and then we'll be able to get a better idea.'

'Okay,' I said amiably. I knew I wasn't coming back, why burst his bubble?

'Good luck up there today, Captain,' Dr Burger said with a friendly smile. 'I'll be rooting for a record breaking flight.'

'Me too,' I replied grimly.

'And be careful.'

'I will,' I said. Oh boy, would I! 'See ya' round the schoolyard, Doc,' I said with a bravado I was far from feeling. Then I winked, and walked out of the office.

I strolled through the hangar and out into the sunshine, blinking at the sudden contrast between the darkness of the hangar and the brilliant light outside. I chuckled to myself as I thought about the answers the doctors would soon be puzzling over. Then I looked at the huge Superfortress standing on the tarmac and realized that would probably be my last laugh for a long time. Perhaps my last laugh ever.

Never mind, I told myself, you just can't think about that right now. Al said he would be here and help you pull this off. All you have to do is trust him and . . . just do it. Hah, another, more cynical part of me thought – trusting Albert and flying a plane, now *that* sounds easy. Well, having a dialogue with myself wasn't going to accomplish anything, either.

It was still very early in the morning, but it was obvious the temperature was going to soar today. The heat waves were already beginning to shimmer off the tarmac and the gleaming metal of the plane. I watched with trepidation as the technicians hurried around the two crafts, carefully cradling and winching the little X-2 in place beneath the Superfortress. For a journey into Never Never land, this was all suddenly becoming far too real for my taste: I was going up in that thing, and I was going to drop into thin air in that thing.

'Jesus,' I muttered under my breath. But of course, I realized that there was no turning back now. Faced with the terrifying prospect of what lay before me, all I could do was fake it, and I knew I had two ways I could play it out; like John Wayne. Or like Woody Allen.

I straightened my shoulders and began a hesitant march forward; I had the feeling that anyone looking at me right now would see the Duke in my stride . . . and Woody's anxiety written all over my face.

Bird Dog suddenly appeared from nowhere and fell into a matched step beside me. 'How ya' doin', Pard?' he asked.

I just nodded in reply. We walked on in silence for a moment.

'Bill . . .' I said finally. 'I want to ask you something.'

'Anything, Pard,' Bird Dog replied casually. 'What is it?'

I took a deep breath. 'What . . . what if I told you I couldn't fly?' I glanced sideways at him, trying to gauge his reaction.

Bill was silent for a few moments, then he gazed over at me, real concern showing in his eyes. 'I'd believe you,' he said seriously.

Part of me felt such deep relief I wanted to burst out crying, hug Bird Dog, generally freak him out with archetypically non-fifties behavior. But the other part of me, the warning-bell part, screamed no! Schmuck! Don't do it! Remember what Al told you: if anyone even *suspects* that you aren't really Captain Tom Stratton, you may never, never leap back . . .

I marched on in grim silence, torn between the two conflicting choices. Then I summoned up every bit of machismo I could and flashed what I hoped would pass for a John Wayne grin. I pointed my trigger finger at him and said, 'Gotcha, Pilgrim.'

Bird Dog stopped dead in his tracks. He blinked in surprise, then burst out laughing. 'You son of a bitch!' he exclaimed.

'Boy, am I good,' I said in a self-congratulatory manner.

'Listen up, Pard,' he grinned, 'Don't you go forgettin' that I'm the one protectin' your ass in the chaser today, so don't go givin' me a hard time, or I'm liable to let you get real nervous up there before I come to your rescue.' He grinned. '*Real* nervous,' he repeated emphatically.

So Bird Dog was flying the F-86. I guessed that was . . . good. In a superstitous sort of way, that is, because in reality, none of it would matter a tinker's damn once I was up in the air. We arrived at the Superfortress, and Bird Dog turned off to the left, towards where the chaser was waiting on a parallel runway. Then he turned back. 'Hey, Pard?'

'Uh huh?' I said, gazing up at the big B-50 looming over me.

Bird Dog gave me a light punch on the arm. 'Get up there and kick some ass today, you hear?'

I mustered a smile. 'I hear,' I said.

He threw me a mock salute, then veered off towards his plane. Before I started up into the B-50, I looked around the runway, but Al wasn't anywhere to be found. You better be up there, buddy, I said silently, or I'm dead meat. Then I took a deep breath, and began the long climb up into the plane.

Inside the cavernous belly, the technicians were busy making last minute adjustments to the X-2, checking the hatch, the landing gear, other equipment which, of course, was completely unfamiliar to me. Hah, I thought, the landing gear – I wanted to tell them they could just skip that part, I wasn't going to need it; instead, I walked around the little plane, stroking its needle nose, acting as if climbing into that toy death-trap was an everyday occurrence for me. What I was really doing was looking around to see where Al might be loitering, but I couldn't spot that telltale rumpled demeanor or impish grin anywhere in the darkness of that big bay.

'Hey, Captain Stratton . . .' It was the quiet balding technician I had spoken to on that first flight.

'Yes . . .' I said, pretending distraction as a cover for not knowing his name.

'We're all rooting for you, sir,' he said. The other technicians nodded and murmured agreements.

'Thanks, boys,' I said, flashing the Duke's grin. 'Keep up the good thoughts, because I'm beginning to think today's the day.'

I gave them the thumbs up, and clambered forward towards the cockpit. 'Al, psst . . .' I hissed.

'Did you say something, Captain?' one of the technicians called after me.

'Just clearing my throat,' I said. Where *was* that damned hologram?

'Hey, Tommy,' Tony LaMott greeted me casually from the pilot's seat. Doug Walker, flying co-pilot, was studying the gauges on the panel in front of him, and gave me a silent wave.

'Hey, guys,' I replied, with just the right touch of casual bravado.

'You ready, Tom?' asked Doug, studying a gauge.

'Oh, sure,' I said. Just something I do every day, my casual tone implied.

I crouched between their seats just the way I had seen Tony do, as the engines roared into life and we began our lumbering roar down the runway. This is it, I thought, my heart beating wildly. Tony nosed the big Superfortress up into the air. I glanced around. No Al. I bit my lip.

The radio crackled into life, and Bird Dog's voice burst melodically through the air. 'Oh, what a beautiful morning . . .'

Tony and Doug laughed. Even I had to smile.

'I gotta beautiful feeling, everything's goin' my way . . .' warbled Bird Dog.

Weird Ernie's voice boomed over the air. 'Including a court martial if you don't clear this radio immediately, Captain.'

'That's a roger, Edwards,' Bird Dog replied cheerfully.

We were climbing steeply, now, and I caught a glimpse of the chaser plane off to the side. It was nice to know that Bird Dog took his work – saving my ass – so seriously. It was unfortunate that unless that damned Al put in an appearance very quickly, Bird Dog wouldn't even get the chance to think he was doing his job.

'Okay . . . looks like it's time to mount up, Tom,' Doug told me casually.

I nodded. Then I took a deep breath and started for the back.

'Hey, Tom . . .' Tony had reached back, and put a restraining hand on my arm. He frowned. 'I know this is going to sound a little strange, but right before I got the fire warning light last trip . . . I could swear I smelled coffee brewing.'

'Coffee?' I blinked. Then I shrugged. 'Maybe it was one of Weird Ernie's gremlins.'

Tony chuckled. 'Yeah, maybe.'

How ironic, I thought, here I was reassuring an experienced test pilot that *he* wasn't crazy, when I was the one who was the *real* candidate for the men with the butterfly nets. I made my way through the narrow passage between the cockpit and the bomb bay. The X-2 sat there awaiting me.

I took a deep breath. There were still three or four technicians fooling around with it . . . but no Albert. I glanced hopefully past the X-2, to the dangerous area in back where Al had perched during the last drop. There was no hint of his presence there, either. What was I going to do?

'Okay, Captain Stratton,' said one of the technicians with revolting cheerfulness. 'Come on over, we'll get you tucked in.'

Tucked in. Great choice of words, I thought grimly. Tucked in for the big final . . . sleep.

'Ah . . . gotta hit the head first,' I said, buying a minute or two.

I raced to the claustrophobic little bathroom at the back of the Superfortress, checking every dark nook and cranny for any sign of that goddammed hologram along the way. Not a trace.

'Damn you, Al, damn you, damn you!' I realized the technicians must be wondering just how I thought I was going to accomplish the task at hand, zipped up tightly in the pressure suit, but frankly, it was the least of my worries at the moment.

Locked in that little head, I found myself saying a fervent prayer. It was a prayer to Albert to get his rear end here, and *now* . . . and I knew if that conscienceless little monster did show up, I would have a hard time not strangling him. Actually, I reflected wildly, I wouldn't *really* have a hard time not strangling him, because I couldn't really touch him!

Okay, enough hysterics, I told myself firmly. I couldn't put off the inevitable any longer: this was it. I emerged from the bathroom and marched grimly to the waiting X-2. I pulled on my helmet and fastened the straps.

Then I took a deep breath, climbed in and hunkered down in the tiny, one-man cockpit as if I had been doing it for years. I thought I kept up a good, casual demeanor as the technicians strapped me in, but inside, I was saying 'Albert,' over and over. Some dying words, I thought irreverently. Then the clear canopy closed down over me and sealed with an ominous whoosh. Oh, God, I thought, what am I going to do?

I attempted to busy myself studying the gauges and dials in front of me, but they might as well have been the controls to a Martian spaceship for all their familiarity. The clock ticked down towards 9:30.

The radio in the X-2 crackled into life. 'Edwards,' I heard Tony say. 'Mother Hen. Level at twenty-five thousand.'

Twenty-five thousand! My heart lurched.

'Roger. Mother Hen.' It was Weird Ernie, from his jeep on the field. 'You are clear to drop.'

Clear to drop. The words I never wanted to hear. I rested my head forward on the instrument panel, feeling dizzy and terrified.

Then I heard a sound which in any other circumstances would have made me smile. It was the faint clank of Weird Ernie rapping on the metal plate in his head.

'Good luck,' he said softly.

Oh boy.

'Ten . . . nine . . .' It was Tony's voice, the voice of doom, counting down to my drop.

'Albert?' I said hopefully.

'. . . eight . . . seven . . .'

He couldn't just abandon me like this. 'Albert!' I said more sharply. 'Goddam it, stop fooling around! We don't have time for this!'

'. . . four . . . three . . .'

No Albert. No joke. I was going to die. I resigned

myself to the fact. I was going to die, and I didn't even know my last name, or what I did for a living, or how old I was.

'. . . two . . . one . . .' Tony's voice boomed.

How utterly pitiful.

'. . . and bombs away!'

Resignation gave way again to utter panic. 'Al!' I screamed, as I felt the X-2 shift, then drop like a rock out of the belly of the Superfortress. I saw air go rushing by me, I saw . . . nothing.

I don't know how many heart-stopping seconds passed before I heard Bird Dog's voice over the radio. 'X-2. Chase One. Do you have a problem?'

Do I have a problem? I wanted to laugh wildly, but I couldn't. I didn't even know how to operate the radio, but I screamed out anyway, the last shriek of a doomed man. 'I can't fly!'

'Relax,' said Albert. 'I can.'

'Al!' I screamed again. Then, 'Where are you?'

'Right here,' he said calmly. And he suddenly materialized right over me – through me. Something. Once the overwhelming panic subsided a little, it was the creepiest feeling. There was my body, there was Al's translucent one, kind of superimposed over me, like double exposure or something. I know that in real time, all this must have happened in a flash, a nano-second; but it seemed as if time was moving like molasses.

I watched with fascination as his see-through arm extended right out – seemingly – of my own body. 'Follow my lead,' he said.

Al's transparent fingers danced over the rocket ignition switches in indecision for a moment, then he made a flicking motion towards two of them. 'Go on,' he said impatiently. 'Do it!'

I repeated the action in reality, flipping the toggles he

had mimed flipping. There was a sudden roar and a whoosh! And then the X-2 accelerated so rapidly that I was slammed back into my seat.

'Good,' said Al, his voice full of satisfaction. 'That was the first rocket.'

'Good,' I echoed weakly.

'Kick in the butt, ain't it?' he asked perkily. Then he reached for the control stick. 'Match me,' he said. 'And don't screw up.'

'*Me?*' I said outraged, 'what about . . .'

'Shut up and do this,' Al said.

His hand appeared to pass through the stick as he made a motion of grasping it and moving it back towards us. Like shifting into second gear. I steeled myself, then grasped the control stick and did exactly what he had done. I eased it back until the position of my hand matched Al's. I could feel the nose of the X-2 rise gently, and we began to accelerate again, racing for the heavens.

Well, it seemed as if we had managed to buy me some time here on planet earth. I sighed, felt some of the tension release from me. Then, just as abruptly, I exploded.

'Where the hell were you!?' I yelled at Al.

'Lakers game.'

'*Lakers* game,' I repeated in disbelief.

'Great game,' he assured me. 'It went into overtime. Coop saved their ass again . . . don't you think he's a severely under-rated player?'

I tried to keep my voice from shaking. 'A ball game! I nearly died because you were at a ball game?'

Al seemed offended by my anger. 'Jesus, Sam! It wasn't just a *ball* game. It was a *play-off*!'

CHAPTER FIFTEEN

'If I could lay my hands on you,' I said through clenched teeth, 'if I could actually touch that transparent apparition that's screwing with my life this way, I'd strangle you!'

'Well, that wouldn't be too smart, now would it?' Al enquired in a maddeningly condescending tone. Because he was actually superimposed over my body, I could feel rather than see his snide little grin; but I would have laid odds that it was there. 'Who'd fly the plane, then?'

'A ball game . . .' I muttered. 'A goddammed ball game, and I'm up here ready to . . .'

The radio crackled suddenly into life, and I heard Bird Dog's laconic voice. 'X-2. Chaser One. You're lookin' good now. What was the problem, Pard?'

'It wasn't my fault, Sam,' Al said reasonably. 'I couldn't help it. Buffy wanted Magic's autograph – I mean, what's a guy supposed to do?'

I sat there, seething.

Al suddenly became all business. His transparent hand tapped silently at a switch on the console. 'Flip that.' I did as I was told. 'Tell him the starting circuit overloaded and you had to recycle. And don't forget to use the correct call words.'

'Don't be so damned patronizing,' I snapped as I flipped the toggle switch. 'Uh . . . Chase One. X-2. I had to recycle the starting circuit. It . . . uh, was overloaded.' Then I hissed at Al. 'Buffy wanted Magic's autograph . . . ' I mimicked him. 'That's truly sick!'

'X-2?' Bird Dog's voice was puzzled. 'Understand that the starting circuit overloaded, Pard. But say again the second part, something about magic or . . . what? Did you say you got *sick*?'

Oh, great, I thought, mentally slapping myself, of course: Bird Dog could hear my half, and my half only, of the conversation with Al. I would have to be *really* careful with that switch. 'Chase One. Scratch that.' I hastily flipped the switch into the off position, and fell back, exhausted.

Al seemed to regain his normal cheerful, self-satisfied equilibrium, and I was forced to listen to him babble on in relentless detail about the wonders of the nearly deadly (for me) play-off game, Coop's miraculous three pointer that pulled them out of a six-minute non-scoring slump, and the detailed points of interest on the lovely Buffy's physical topography.

Luckily for Al – and for me – all the time he was rambling on about his exploits, he also continued to show me where to press, where to pull, where to switch and when to talk. We were climbing higher and higher into a cloudless heaven, and as the speed kept increasing in measured increments, I responded to the radio requests, and obediently read the numbers off to Weird Ernie waiting below. That is, I responded immediately after Al told me what to say.

'Mach point eight. All readings in the green,' I said, parroting Al perfectly. I flipped the switch to the off position. 'Thanks so much for sharing, Al,' I said sarcastically. 'The victory party really sounds like lots of fun.'

'Oh, it was,' he replied gleefully; he apparently missed the sarcastic inflection in my voice. 'It really was. It's too bad you couldn't have been there,' he added thoughtfully.

'Yeah. And gee . . . I guess, considering your rather

late appearance here at all, I suppose I should really count my blessings that you didn't decide to put a perfect capper on the whole wonderful evening by spending the night with Buffy!'

There was a moment of awkward silence.

'My God!' I said, stunned. 'I don't believe you! I'm about to plunge to my death, and you get distracted by boffing someone named *Buffy*!'

Al pointed at the radio switch, and I fumed as I turned it on.

'Coming up on Mach one,' he said meekly.

'Coming up on Mach one,' I repeated through clenched teeth.

The sky deepened in color as we climbed, the blue became more intense, more palpable, and there was a silence in the cockpit, as Al concentrated on the tasks at hand, and I concentrated on mimicking his every move and every word. The feeling of utter isolation was intense.

'Mach one-three,' he said. 'Fifty thousand. Nosing over.'

I echoed the words into the mike.

Al's hand moved forward, and with a surprisingly delicate motion, eased slowly through the control stick. I followed the motion, matching it perfectly, but actually moving the stick, with my hand.

'You're getting the knack of this,' Al observed, pleased.

I shrugged. 'You know what they say about necessity being . . . well, anyway.'

'You're mixing your metaphors again, Sam,' Al said jauntily.

'Again?' I asked curiously.

'You always did.' Al seemed to regret the offhanded personal remark – it must have been on the Ziggy list of no-nos – and immediately changed the subject. 'See what's happening with the plane right now?'

I looked around. Sky, more sky. It all looked vaguely the same to me. 'No,' I said. 'What's happening?'

'Oy, Sam! Look – we're still climbing, even though the nose is beginning to come down.' He paused and pointed at the mike. 'Mach one-seven. Fifty-six thousand.'

'Mach one-seven,' I echoed, 'fifty-six thousand.' I switched the mike off. 'What does that mean, what you just said?'

'And your syntax is going to hell in a handbasket, too,' he said.

'Al, for Christ's sake! This is hardly the time for grammar lessons.'

He sighed patiently. 'It means we are starting to level off, Sam.'

'Oh,' I said blankly.

Al pointed to the mike. 'Level at seventy thousand. Mach two-four. On profile.'

I repeated his words and clicked off the mike.

'Look,' Al said, and pointed.

Where there had been just endless sky and nothing else, now there *was* something else visible: through the clear little bubble of a cockpit I could actually see the curvature of the earth. I sucked in my breath as if I had been punched in the gut.

'My God,' I said, awe-struck by the sight. 'That's incredible.'

'Yeah,' Al agreed. 'It is.'

We flew on in compatible silence for a few moments, and I used the quiet interim to study that once-in-a-lifetime view; it was like all the 'National Geographics' and computerized graphics space age reports I had ever seen, all rolled into one. It was like a kid's dream come true, a guest appearance in a 'Star Wars' movie, and I was here in it, an actual observer. Maybe all of this confusion and chaos and terror had been worth it, after all.

'Sam,' Al's sober voice broke unexpectedly into my reverie.

'Hmm?' I said, still distracted by the beauty and wonder before me.

He paused and actually seemed to sigh. 'I have to tell you something.'

Uh-oh. 'What is it?' I asked.

'A little glitch came up since I saw you last . . .'

'A little glitch?' I echoed.

'The research should have gone deeper, earlier,' Al said reluctantly, 'when Ziggy was first checking into the history of this flight.'

'What's the bad news, Al?' I said, steeling myself.

'They never found out what set off those fire warning lights.'

'Keep going,' I said grimly.

'Whatever it was, it wasn't a false alarm,' Al said. 'Tom Stratton was killed when this bird we're flying blew up breaking Mach three.'

'But . . . you told me in order to "Quantum leap," I *have* to break Mach three,' I said, confused.

'I know,' Al said. 'The problem is, we don't know what the problem *was*. They scrapped the project after you, after Tom Stratton . . .'

'Oh, Jesus,' I said.

'Yeah,' Al agreed. 'But of course,' he added hopefully, 'that's just the way Ziggy has it computed.'

'What?' I joked, 'no odds?'

Al was silent.

'Whew,' I said softly, and stared out into space. Beautiful, deadly space. So this was it. My guest appearance was a one-shot deal. There really *wasn't* any way for me to get back – not unless I broke Mach three, which was exactly what had killed the real Tom Stratton. The dream was about to turn into a full fledged nightmare, the kind where you don't wake up at the end.

'You think it's worth the risk, Al?'

'I don't really see a choice, Sam,' he said honestly. 'I know you, and I know as well as you do that you can't stick around in someone else's life. I figure you'd want to go for broke – maybe we can figure the solution out together. Am I wrong?'

I thought about it for a moment. The horizon curved off into infinity before me. I thought about the dreams I'd had, the rolling banks of clouds, the ascension to greater heights than I had imagined existed, and the plunge back to earth.

I thought about Peg and Mikey, and I thought about my own father, although he was still just a dim picture in my mind. Whatever I had been doing in the future, whatever it was that had led me to this point, I had to just . . . keep on doing it. I didn't see a choice either, not really.

'No, Al,' I said, 'you aren't wrong.'

'Okay,' he said calmly. 'Then this is it, kid. Seize the day.'

His ghostly finger passed through the third engine toggle, the third rocket which would take me through Mach three, or to my death.

I reached forward hesitantly, touched the toggle with the tip of my finger, then withdrew it. Then I took a deep breath and put my hand forward again, and flipped the switch.

There was a roar like nothing I had ever heard before, as the third engine ignited, and the needle-nose rocket leaped forward into space.

Al gave an unexpected little whoop! of glee. 'Ain't this a kick in the ass?' he said.

Easy for him: no matter what happened next, he was

going to materialize, body parts intact, wherever he had come from.

'Whatever happens, Al . . .' I said. 'I just want to tell you . . .'

'Oh, don't go all sentimental on me,' he said, annoyed. 'You did the right thing.' But I could tell he was touched by the idea.

'I just want to tell you,' I repeated firmly, 'that if I die in this crash, I hope to God the Lakers lose in seven.'

'Sam!' Al sounded shocked at such blasphemy.

'Every year,' I added.

I heard the radio static, then Bird Dog's voice filtered into the cockpit. 'X-2. Chase one. I'm down here watchin' your butt, Pard.'

I flipped the switch. 'Chase One. How do we look?'

'X-2. Dynamite.' Bird Dog's voice sounded cheerfully normal.

Weird Ernie promptly broke in. 'Chase One. Edwards. Get the hell off the radio. Right now!'

Bird Dog fired his parting shot. 'X-2. Ride 'em, cowboy!' he said, then his voice was gone.

Al's see-through hand pointed at the speed gauge, then the temperature gauge, then the radio. 'Mach two-seven,' he said. 'Skin temperature seven-fifty.'

I repeated the words to Weird Ernie as we streaked along.

'Mach two-eight,' said Al.

'Mach two-eight,' I said. Then I heard the most peculiar sound, a popping sort of a noise. At first, I couldn't place it or identify it. 'Do you hear something?' I asked Al.

'Mach two-nine,' said Al. 'Yes.'

'Mach two-nine,' I said automatically. 'Oh, Jesus!'

The red fire warning light suddenly began to flash in an insistent, ominous blink; within a second, the alarm began to ring. So this was it, I thought, the end of the line. The peculiar bubbling noise continued to grow in intensity, and all of a sudden, I remembered something Tony LaMott had said about coffee . . .

'Al! Tony thought he smelled coffee – he didn't *smell* it! He *heard* it, perking!'

'Holy . . .' Al said. 'That's it! It's the fuel! The heat of the plane is actually boiling the fuel!' For the first time, he sounded panicked. He pointed furiously at the switches. 'Shut down, Sam!'

I hesitated.

'Damn it, Sam! Shut it down!' His ghostly fingers were actually going through the motions, trying to shut the switches off, shut the plane down. But of course, he was a hologram – he couldn't really touch the equipment. He couldn't stop the plane.

I still hesitated. It was so crazy, but I couldn't take my eyes off the speed gauge. The needle crept agonizingly slowly up from Mach two-nine. It hovered right in the middle, trembling, then moved a fraction of an inch to the right.

'Sam, God damn it, shut this thing down or you're going to die!' Al yelled.

A mini-fraction more . . . 'We've got to hit Mach three,' I yelled back, over the noise of the engines and the blaring of the alarm.

'You can't!' he screamed.

'I *can*!' I said. It was more of a prayer than a statement of fact.

The perking sound was growing louder, and I knew – without really knowing – that any moment the X-2 was going to just explode in mid-air. My knuckles were white with the effort of not reaching for the switches.

'Sam!' Al was screaming my name over and over, but it was as if he wasn't there. It was as if nothing mattered any more, nothing except getting that needle to the highest point it has ever been, breaking Mach three . . .

My eyes were riveted on that gauge. Come on, I thought, come on! Just a little more to the right and . . . and it did!

'Now, Sam!' Al screamed, his fingers scrabbling furiously at the ejection button by the side of my seat. 'Do it!'

I put my finger on the button, closed my eyes, and pushed. There was a roar and a whoosh, as the clear cockpit bubble popped open, and I was propelled into mid-air, suspended eerily for a moment before I began a plummet to earth.

'Pull the damned rip cord!' I heard Al's voice, and realized that he was still with me, even on the fall. 'There!'

I fumbled for it, and found a length of nylon hanging from the harness that held me. I yanked hard, and my plummet stopped abruptly with a sickeningly jarring whoomph! Then I was floating in air, and it was just like my childhood dreams and the dreams I'd had the last few nights, all wrapped up in one. I watched, entranced, as the air lightened, and clouds appeared. Then I actually descended through the masses of clouds – which had a distinct clammy feeling, and were nothing at all like the benevolent puffballs of imagination.

This is it, I thought triumphantly. This is it. I broke Mach three. I did it!

'Hey, Al,' I said, eager to share my happiness with him. But he had disappeared again. Amazing, the way he could just . . . do that. Well, I thought, I would see him again. Where we both belonged.

With surprising speed, I saw the brown of the earth below, rushing up to meet me, and realized that I was travelling a lot faster than the leisurely pace I had thought I was going at.

Then the ground was there, and I had no time to try to change my position or cushion my landing. There was a sudden lurch and crash, and miles of white silk floated down around me as everything went black . . .

*   *   *

There was a sound, and it was really annoying. But try as I might, I couldn't seem to figure out exactly what it might be. It was a clamoring, wailing sound, and it went on and on and on. It seemed to be . . . far away. Then it seemed to be . . . moving closer. What was that again? It was familiar. I struggled to put a name to it, but nothing would come.

I sneezed and opened my eyes. There was dust on my face and in my nose, and there was billowing white silk all around me. I struggled uncomfortably up onto one elbow and attempted to untangle myself from the fabric prison. What the hell had happened, I wondered, my mind a blank. I shook my head to clear it, and felt heat rising in waves all around me. Gingerly, I pushed the silk aside and peered out.

I was surrounded by cracked, dry desert – a barren, inhospitable place that seemed, nevertheless, familiar. And the wailing sound that had seemed familiar as well, I realized with a start, was the sound of sirens. In the shimmering distance, I could make out the traveling vehicles that were headed my way. Ambulances, I thought, taking stock of my surroundings. I . . . fell. No. I parachuted. To the desert. And there were ambulances coming for me.

All of a sudden, I realized where I was. And worse, who I was. 'Oh, no!' I said softly, a plea. 'God damn it, no!'

The vehicles kicked up voluminous dust clouds; they seemed to criss-cross each other in the hallucinatory distance, and then they resolved themselves into recognizable shapes. And as they approached, I became certain that what I had suspected was true.

They screeched to an abrupt halt, and I saw Weird Ernie and Dr Burger clamber out of one of the jeeps and race towards me. From an ambulance behind them, uniformed men began to unload a stretcher.

'Tom!' Dr Burger shouted as he raced towards me, 'Tom, are you all right?'

'Thank God,' said Weird Ernie, standing over me. He looked tremendously relieved.

'Thank God?' I echoed dully. 'Why?'

He stared at me in surprise. 'Well, Captain Stratton,' he said. 'Thank God you're alive.' He pointed off across the desert, and I could just make out wisps of smoke. 'See those smoke signals?'

I nodded.

'Well, those are little pieces, and they're all that's left of the X-2,' he said. 'We didn't know if you'd gotten out in time.'

'You mean, I didn't break Mach three?' I said.

Dr Burger laughed. 'You pilots – you should be happy you're still on the planet.' He looked at me with a kindly smile. 'But, just for the record, congratulations. You *did* break Mach three!'

'But then why am I still here?' I wailed plaintively.

The doctors exchanged glances and shrugged.

'Shock,' Dr Burger said softly.

Weird Ernie nodded. 'Concussion?' he asked. Dr Burger shrugged.

I could have told them differently, but then, it probably was shock. Not the kind they had in mind, but shock nevertheless.

'Come on, Tom,' Dr Burger said, 'let's take a look at that noggin of yours – maybe you got a bump or something.'

I allowed myself to be put on a stretcher and carried to a waiting ambulance. What else could I do? Was I ever going to get out of this place?

CHAPTER SIXTEEN

'For God's sake, stop fussing over me! I'm perfectly capable of sitting up!' I said crossly as I unbuckled the straps that bound my chest to the stretcher on which I had been carried to the ambulance, and struggled into an upright position.

'Take it easy, Tom, this is just routine,' Dr Burger said calmly.

I wanted to scream, 'And that's another thing – there is absolutely nothing routine about this and I'm *not* Tom, God damn it!' but I knew that he would only chalk it up to the ravings of a man who had just fallen to earth out of an exploding airplane.

Dr Burger approached me with a slim penlight in one hand, and began to check my eyes. I stared grimly ahead while the thin beam went to the left, then the right.

'You know,' Dr Burger said conversationally, 'you really should be a little happier. After all, you broke the record . . . and besides, from the hunks of metal that dropped to the ground before you did, we thought by now we'd be combing the desert with tweezers and glass jars, just looking for what was left of you.' He peered closely into my left eye again, and seemed satisfied. 'Okay, no dilation. Good.'

I sat in sullen silence. Great, I had broken the record. Where did it get me? Right back here.

Dr Burger shook his head. 'You guys are all alike. You act as if losing your plane is as bad as losing your wife.'

'I'd trade *my* ex-wife – actually, any one of my ex-wives

– for any old wreck they've got.' There was no mistaking Al's voice; I glanced up sharply and sure enough, there he was, perched cockily on the edge of an empty stretcher behind Dr Burger, who couldn't see or hear him, anyway. My own personal gremlin.

I squinted angrily at him as Dr Burger turned and rummaged around in his bag. 'I'm still here,' I told Al in a tight voice.

'Yes, you are,' Dr Burger agreed. 'And it's about time you realized how lucky you are,' he added, without glancing up.

Great, I thought. But at that point, I just didn't give a damn any more. Let him listen. 'What now?' I asked Al.

'Now I'm going to take your blood pressure,' Dr Burger said matter of factly. This peculiar three way conversation seemed to somehow be working on its own level.

'Well,' said Al, 'I suppose we could always try the A-bomb theory.'

'No, thank you,' I replied icily.

Dr Burger turned around with the cuff in his hand. 'I'm sorry, Tom, but it's procedure. Lie back down, please.'

Disgruntled, I did as I was told, and Dr. Burger strapped the old-fashioned cuff around my upper arm and began to pump.

'After all, it wasn't even my theory, Sam.' It was Al's voice again. 'I never did buy into that good-deed-put-time-right bullshit.'

I snorted in derision.

'Not really, anyway,' Al added weakly.

'So I'm just stuck here,' I said accusingly.

Dr Burger frowned at the blood pressure dial. 'Oh, I don't think so,' he said. 'You look fine so far. We'll just run a few simple tests at the hospital and then you can go home.'

Home, I thought depressed. Right.

'Maybe not,' Al said. 'Maybe . . . you'll just leap right back when you least expect it. Like tonight, when you're asleep.' His voice held that false-cheery note, the kind people use when they are trying to convince a sick kid that the shot won't *really* hurt.

'You don't really believe that,' I snapped.

Dr Burger stared at me, surprised. 'Well, of course I do,' he said reasonably. 'I certainly don't see any reason to keep you in the hospital.'

I sighed.

'Anyway, while we're still working on the problem,' Al said, 'there's nothing I can do here.' He glanced down at his watch, then back up at me. 'Besides, the second play-off game begins in a half-hour.'

I almost lunged off the stretcher at him.

'On the other hand,' Dr Burger said, frowning at the blood pressure gauge, 'if your blood pressure keeps elevating like this, I might want you to spend the night for observation.'

'I'll be fine,' I assured him. 'Really.'

'This is awfully erratic,' he said, puzzled.

'I'll just bet,' I said grimly. I looked up to give Al the evil-eye, but naturally, he was gone. Leaving me here again, in 1956 in someone else's life.

'Okay,' said Dr Burger, pulling out a little mallet, 'let's check your reflexes.'

I played the obedient patient all the way to the hospital, and according to Dr Burger, everything seemed to check out fine. Of course, he hadn't mentioned the memory test yet; and I shuddered to think what kind of lame yet plausible excuse I would have to come up with to explain the answers I had given. Maybe I would wind up in the looney bin, after all. I was getting very depressed just thinking about the infinite possibilities for the future – all bleak – when we finally pulled up to the hospital.

It was another one of those flat, featureless buildings that had sprung up in the desert area for strictly utilitarian reasons. The hospital looked as if it had been dropped, fully constructed, from some cheesy Army surplus store. Dr Burger opened the door and motioned me onto the stretcher, but I shook my head.

'I'm fine,' I said firmly. 'I can walk.'

The sunlight was bright and hot – the predicted scorcher had developed with a vengeance – and everything was just as I had left it. Jesus. I shook my head in disgust, as we pushed through the double doors into the hospital. Just inside the corridor, I saw a small boy with a baseball glove come flying towards me.

'Daddy!' he said, leaping into my arms. 'I heard your plane . . .' his voice was frightened.

'Mikey!' I exclaimed, surprised. I hugged him. 'Hey, no problem! I'm okay. Really I am. See?'

'Really?' he asked tremulously.

'Really,' I assured him. 'What are you doing here, anyway?'

Then, over Mikey's head, I spotted Sally and Lucy, huddled together, staring at us. I felt a pang of anxiety rush through me. 'What happened, Mikey?' I asked gently. 'Is it . . . mom?'

Dr Burger hurried over from a brief conference with a nurse. 'Tom,' he said gently, 'it's Peg. She went into premature labor when she heard the crash.'

I remembered the fright on Peg's face when Tony buzzed the barbeque. I remembered her assurances that this was the kind of fear all flyers' wives lived with. Damn it, I thought, kicking myself mentally, why had I believed her?

'Is she . . .' I wanted to ask if she was going to lose the baby, if she was all right, but I was suddenly conscious of Mikey's weight in my arms, and I didn't want to frighten him any more than he was already frightened.

Dr Burger nodded over Mikey's head. 'Okay so far,' he said cryptically.

I put Mikey down, then knelt to face him, man to man on his own level. 'Listen, champ,' I said softly, 'I know you want to see your mom. And you will.' Mikey nodded, not fully understanding. 'But right now,' I said, 'what I really need you to do for me is to stay here with Sally and Lucy for a while.' I leaned closer and whispered confidentially, 'See, they're both pregnant, too, and they're scared. You understand?'

I don't know if he really did, but he nodded. 'Yes, sir,' he said softly.

'Good,' I said, brushing my hand over his flat top. 'She'll be okay, son, I promise.' Then I stood up and took Mikey by the hand.

We walked over to where Sally and Lucy were standing. Lucy took Mikey's hand from mine, while Sally gave me a hug. 'Oh, Tom,' she said, then seemed to be unable to say anything more.

I nodded. 'I know. Keep an eye on Mikey for me?' I asked.

'Of course,' she whispered.

I hugged Mikey again, and saw that he was trying to hold back his tears. 'It's okay,' I assured him again, although I didn't know if it was or not.

Then I rushed down the corridor in the direction I had seen Dr Burger take. Outside a half-closed door I spotted Dr Burger talking softly with another white-coated man and a nurse. I flew by them without stopping, and entered the room.

Pcg was lying in a narrow, white-sheeted bed. She was

hooked up to some simplistic looking monitors, and an IV bag dripped something into her slender forearm.

'Oh, Peg,' I said, at a loss for words.

But her face, deathly pale and glistening with a fine sheen of perspiration, lit up when she saw me.

'Tom!' She held out her arms, and I sat on the edge of the bed. She hugged me tightly. 'Oh,' she said, a tear trickling down her cheek, 'I just knew you'd keep your promise!'

And that's when I understood what she had asked me to promise last night – that I would come back safely – and I tried to smile. 'So that's what it was,' I said.

'Of course,' she said, hugging me tightly again.

'It would take more than one of Weird Ernie's gremlins to kill me,' I assured her.

'Tough guy,' Peg murmured. Then she looked up at me. 'Did you set a record?' she asked.

'I guess I did,' I shrugged.

'Oh, Tom!' Peg said happily. 'I'm so proud of you!'

I touched her hospital issue gown. 'Guess they wouldn't let you wear your baby dolls, huh?'

Peg shook her head, then her face clouded. 'No,' she said softly. 'No baby dolls, maybe no baby.'

'Oh, honey . . .' I said helplessly. I wanted so badly to do something, to help in some way.

Then I saw her wince with pain. 'Contraction?' I said.

Peg nodded silently. I held her lightly and ran my hand over her fine blonde hair.

'Look at me,' I said. 'Take a deep breath. Like this.' I had no idea where the words or the knowledge of what to do were coming from.

Peg took a deep breath.

'Hold it,' I said, 'then let it out, like this.' I released my breath in short, staccato puffs, and Peg watched me closely, then mimicked the action.

The pain actually seemed to let up, and she smiled wanly at me. 'I guess the baby hasn't gotten the word yet that everything is okay.'

I squeezed her hand reassuringly. 'Well, we'll just have to get it to him. Her.'

'We'd better,' said Peg. 'I haven't even bought the layette yet.'

I glanced over my shoulder and saw that the doctors' conference in the hall was still going on. 'I'll be right back,' I said to Peg, giving her a light kiss on the forehead, 'I want to talk to the doctor.'

Out in the glare of the stark hallway, I joined Dr Burger and the other doctor.

'Tom,' Dr. Burger said, 'this is Doctor Blaustein.'

We shook hands. 'How does it look?' I asked bluntly.

Dr Blaustein shook his head, his expression grave and sympathetic. 'I'm afraid it doesn't look very good, Captain,' he said. 'The baby is going to arrive at least nine weeks premature. The nearest neo-natal unit is in L.A.'

'Let's get her there,' I said.

He held up a cautionary hand. 'We do have a plane standing by, but considering the shock Mrs Stratton's been through, I'm very reluctant to do it. I think the risk is too great.'

I looked from doctor to doctor, trying to figure out just what I was supposed to do.

'It's your decision, Tom,' Dr Burger said gently.

'What do you think?' I asked helplessly.

'I'd recommend delivering here, and then flying the baby to L.A.'

I shook my head. 'The baby won't stand a chance, will it?'

'Not much,' Dr Blaustein said soberly, 'but your wife will.'

163

I turned my head and looked into the room. Peg was watching us, and she gave me a weak smile. My God, I thought, now her life is in my hands, too. Why, oh *why* was this happening to me? I smiled back at her, then turned back to the waiting doctors.

'How far apart are her contractions?' I asked.

Dr Burger looked surprised. Dr Blaustein replied, 'It's very early labor. They're spaced fairly far apart right now.'

'How far is she dilated?' I demanded. Once again, the words were coming out of my mouth without me thinking about them. So this must be . . . Sam . . . talking, I realized with a start, then concentrated on the problem we faced. Both doctors looked very surprised at the question, too.

'Ah . . . two centimeters,' Dr Blaustein told me, 'and the cervix is partially effaced.'

'But . . . then it's early enough to stop it!' I exclaimed happily.

'Captain,' Dr Blaustein said, giving me a very peculiar look, 'once labor has started, I'm afraid there *is* no way to stop it.'

'Of course there is!' I snapped. 'Start her on a beta sympathomimetic!'

Dr Burger stared at me as if I was speaking Latin. 'A what?'

'A beta sympathomimetic,' I repeated impatiently. 'I'm not sure which one, obstetrics isn't my specialty. Probably . . . ritodrine or terbutaline.'

There was an ominous silence in the hallway. 'Oh,' I said with sudden comprehension. 'Of course . . . those didn't come out until the late 70s.'

Dr Burger put a none too gentle hand on my arm. 'Excuse us for a moment,' he said to Dr Blaustein, and pulled me into a nearby room. He closed the door behind us and faced me angrily.

'Captain,' he said through clenched teeth, 'I don't know what the hell you think you're doing, but the *only* reason that I'm not kicking your ass from here to the flight line is that woman across the hall needs you.'

'She doesn't have to deliver,' I insisted. 'Believe me, I know what I'm talking about.' And I did. I didn't know how I knew what I was talking about, but I was certain I did.

'Now you're a doctor?' he snapped at me.

'Evidently,' I said with wonder. I stared over his shoulder at a blank wall, in an attempt to pull my thoughts together.

At that moment, Dr Burger pulled the questionnaire from his pocket. 'Tom,' he said calmly, 'considering what you've been through today, I'm going to make an allowance for your behavior. *Up to now.* But if you persist in wasting our time by continuing this . . .' he waved the questionnaire in front of my face, '. . . this ridiculous *sham* that you and Captain Birdell have cooked up, I'll personally see to it that you never fly again.'

I had nothing to lose. I looked him straight in the eye. 'It isn't a sham,' I told him. 'Every one of those answers are true.'

He turned away in evident disgust. 'Doctor Ernst was right,' he said, 'you're one sick son of a bitch.'

I grabbed him by the arm and whirled him around to face me. 'Listen. Ethonol alcohol,' I said rapidly. 'A five per cent solution of ethonol alcohol in dextrose and water intravenously administered will stop labor.' I took a breath and plunged on before he could speak. 'The technique was developed in the sixties. Beta sympatho-mimetics replaced it in the seventies, but it'll still work!'

Dr Burger looked at me as if I was the lowest form of vermin he had ever encountered. He tried to break free of my grasp, but I just held on tighter.

'Use your *brain*, dammit!' I said. 'What will an intravenous five per cent solution of alcohol *do?*'

'Get her instantly drunk!' he replied contemptuously.

'And?' I said.

'And . . .' Then his eyes widened as he followed the thought to its logical conclusion. 'Oh my . . . and that will interfere with the oxytocins her brain is releasing to stimulate uterine contractions!'

'Thank you,' I said with a relieved sigh.

He stared at me in complete bewilderment for a second, hurried from the room, and huddled in quick conference with Dr Blaustein. I saw Blaustein shrug disbelievingly, then look at me and ask Dr Burger something. I walked back out into the hallway.

'I don't have the foggiest idea,' I heard Dr Burger say. 'But it's worth . . .'

The conversation ended, and I could see Blaustein huddle in another fast consultation, this one with the nurse who had been there before. A few minutes later, a new solution was brought into Peg's room, and they replaced her IV with a bottle of clear liquid.

'Okay, Peg,' I heard Dr Blaustein say soothingly, 'we're going to try something new.'

'Where's Tom?' she asked.

'Right here, honey,' I waved from my post in the hallway. 'The doctors want me to stay out for a couple of minutes until the . . . until this new stuff starts to take effect.'

And a few minutes it was, if even that long. I was staring at the shiny linoleum when I heard an off-key warbling emerge from Peg's room.

'*Que sera, sera* . . .' she sang. 'Whatever will be, will be. The future's not ours to see. *Que sera, sera,* what will be, *sera* . . .' She broke off and grinned crookedly at the doctors. 'Hey, guys, what do you think?'

Dr Burger actually laughed. 'We have Doris Day for a patient,' he said.

'Ah hah!' Peg said, 'No! You have . . . Eliza Dolittle!' And with that, she broke into a squeaky rendition of 'Wouldn't It Be Loverly', complete with terrible cockney accent.

She seemed to be thoroughly amusing herself, and the doctors emerged from the room looking pleased, but puzzled.

'Well?' I demanded.

They exchanged glances and shrugged.

'She's going to have one hell of a hangover,' Dr Blaustein said, 'but she's not going to deliver.' He paused for a moment. 'Now, Captain Stratton, would you mind telling me how the hell . . .'

Dr Burger looked from me to Blaustein to Peg, then shook his head at my silence. 'Do me a favor, Barry,' he said to Dr Blaustein, 'just don't ask.'

As Dr Blaustein turned wearily and trudged down the hallway, Dr Burger turned to me. 'And I suppose,' he said tentatively, '*I* shouldn't ask, either.'

I smiled at him and shrugged. 'You have the right, Doc,' I replied. 'I'm going to visit with Peg.' And I headed into her room before he could ask anything else.

Peg looked completely crocked and very happy to see me again. 'Hey, flyboy,' she said with a slurry giggle, 'the squares are gone. Gone, gone.' She grinned slyly. 'Wanna boogie?'

I laughed and sat beside her on the edge of the bed. She pulled me to her and gave me a long, sloppy, sweet kiss.

'I love you, flyboy,' she said.

I looked into her dizzy blue eyes. 'I love you too, Peg.' And I meant it.

She sighed happily. 'I know,' she said, and put her

head back against the pillow. In an instant, she had fallen asleep, knocked out by the alcohol. I gazed down at her, fondness and anxiety mixing in my feelings. Well, I thought, at least the baby was safe. I kissed her gently on the forehead, and got up.

I walked over to the open window and stared out at the desert and the mountains beyond. It was beautiful, and I supposed I had better start getting used to the view. I saw someone waving to get my attention, and shifted my glance downward to where Mikey was standing with Bird Dog. He must have hurried to the hospital as soon as he heard about Peg.

Bird Dog cocked a questioning eyebrow at me, and I nodded. I gave Mikey a thumb's up and smiled. 'Mom's okay,' I told him. 'The baby's okay, too.'

Mikey jumped up and down with relief. Then he gave a whoop, and tossed the baseball he was holding up into the air. To my surprise, the ball appeared to make a curve, and head straight towards me. I leaned out to catch it, but it seemed to just keep going, up, up, up, in an immense impossible arc.

Then, without any warning, there was a tremendous rushing sound, and darkness descended, blotting everything out – Mikey, Bird Dog, the hospital room. All I could see was the baseball, highlighted in some sort of bright, artificial light, as it dropped, curving downward towards my outstretched arms.

I caught it with a satisfying thump of leather, and then I heard the most peculiar sound. It was as if a crowd was roaring. First I looked down. The baseball was lodged securely in the worn leather glove I was wearing on my right hand. Glove? I thought. Then I looked around. I was staring straight at a set of bleachers, sparsely populated, but noisy. I was standing on a baseball field. And I was wearing a baseball uniform.

Time seemed to freeze. I was utterly dumbfounded.

Then I heard someone yell, 'Whatta you posing for, Fox? Ain't nobody going to take your picture!'

My razor sharp mind went to work. I was in a night game, somewhere, some time. I was no longer Tom Stratton, that much was certain.

I had made the quantum leap, after all. But I had the distinct feeling that Sam whoever I was *wasn't* a baseball player. So . . . it was *a* quantum leap, but it appeared to be the wrong one. Again.

'*Albert!*' I yelled.

CHAPTER SEVENTEEN

'Come on, Foxy, move your butt!'

It was a good-natured order clearly aimed at me. Me, that is, but now someone called Foxy. What could I do? Adaptable guy that I seem to be, I obligingly headed in towards the dugout with the rest of what was apparently my professional baseball team. One part of me was saying, 'This is going to be harder to fake than flying a plane.' Another part of me was reasoning, 'But it's a lot safer.' And a third part was spewing forth an unrepeatable string of invectives aimed at Albert. One thing I could do, it appeared, was develop an on-the-spot multiple personality, complete with conflicting voices.

Some guy trotted past me from left field and slapped me familiarly on the ass. 'Nice catch, Foxy.'

I grinned weakly.

'Yeah,' an old man chimed in from the bleachers, 'a couple more like that and maybe they'll send you up.' Then he laughed raucously.

Well, I had suspected this was minor league, and it looked as if I was right – very minor. When I reached the dugout, I paused, then turned to study the scoreboard. It was the bottom of the ninth, and we, the Waco Bombers, were trailing the visiting Kileen Blue Devils, five-zip.

From the loudspeaker above the thin crowd, the scratchy strains of 'Downtown' blared. Okay, I thought, I've got a lock on this – it's got to be the sixties. I looked hastily around. Uh-huh. Ratted hair and mini skirts. Bell bottoms. Scraggly moustaches. I was right, all right. It wasn't quite as disorienting as the first leap had been – at least I knew what had happened. Sort of, anyway. But what the hell was I *doing* here?

I stood to one side, trying to be as inconspicuous as possible and watched my Waco Bombers teammates slumped on the bench, looking bored and dejected. The team manager, who had 'Pop,' stitched on his blue cap, eyed us with worry. He clapped his hands, a feeble attempt, I guess, to arouse some team spirit.

'Okay, let's go!' he said, spitting a stream of tobacco juice to punctuate his words. 'Let's go! Hustle, I wanna see some hustle!' He spit again. 'We can take these damned Oakies, boys!'

There were a few halfhearted grunts from the players, but mostly, no one seemed to pay much attention to him. He turned a jaundiced eye in my direction. 'Get over here, Foxy,' he said.

As I slunk all the way into the dugout, a mangy fox terrier who had been lying in the dirt scratching himself looked up at me and began to growl. I gave him wide berth and headed for the bench.

Pop shook his head. 'Even Jack's given up,' he said mournfully.

As I seated myself between two players, I realized he was talking about the dog. The animal was now on his feet showing considerably more energy than anyone else in the dugout – his legs were locked in an aggressive stance, and he was staring at me, his furious barking alternating with a menacing growl.

The short stop sitting next to me nudged me. 'Give it to him, Foxy.'

The kid on the other side of me seemed to agree with whatever the short stop was suggesting. 'Pepper's right, Foxy,' he said, 'game's almost over anyway.'

'Yeah,' another player chimed in, 'go on, give it to him.'

'Ah . . . what?' I ventured.

The guys laughed as if I had made a joke, and then the one sitting next to me, the one called Pepper, reached into my pocket and pulled out a Zero candy bar. He dropped it at the terrier's feet, but the dog resolutely ignored it – he was intent on barking at me, and not letting up. I could feel the surprise among the men around me, and scrambled frantically for an explanation. Obviously, I was supposed to know why this was happening.

Luckily, the announcer's voice boomed over the loud speaker just then, providing a few moments of distraction.

'It's Doug Ibold, folks, the voice of the Waco Bombers.'

'Lucky him,' the kid next to me said morosely, but everyone seemed to take a sort of perverse pleasure in listening to the rapid-fire patter, anyway. And the news certainly didn't seem to be good.

'. . . coming to you from WACO 1130 AM, just like always. Well, this is it, folks. Unless the Bombers can pull a miracle out of their collective cap and win this final game of what's been a real disappointment of this sixty-six season . . .'

So I was right about the time.

'. . . it's a winter bunk in the cellar for the third year in a row.'

Jesus, I thought, three years in a row. No wonder that old guy laughed when he made that crack about being sent up to the majors!

'. . . and Pop's huddling with the team in the dugout right now. Barnes, who's oh-for-three, will lead off the middle of the order.' He paused for a breath, then hurried on. 'The bottom of the ninth is brought to you tonight as it has been all year long, by Schneck and Schneck Funeral Parlors, serving Waco and the Texas hill country for forty-three years.'

I heard someone hoot from the stands. 'Couldn't get a more fittin' sponsor for these deadbeats than a funeral parlor!'

I saw Pop wince and try to ignore the jibe. Meanwhile, the obnoxious little terrier was getting more and more hysterical. I saw him bare his fangs at me, and tried to curl back into the bench. Just what I needed, a damned dog drawing attention to me – as if things weren't difficult enough already!

The players closed ranks in a circle around the dog. Pepper, the diminutive short stop, grabbed him by the collar.

'What the hell's gotten into him?' Pepper asked me.

I shrugged helplessly.

'I think he's trying to tell us something,' another one of the players said, puzzled.

Just then, another diversion – in the form of the umpire – presented itself. He pushed his way through the crowd towards Pop. 'Your boys gonna play with the dog or play ball?' he asked genially.

Pop motioned to one of the men. 'Barnes, you're up.'

The one called Barnes walked between me and the dog on his way to the bat rack.

'And Barnes,' Pop said pleadingly, 'try not to swing at the first pitch, okay?'

'I know, I know,' said Barnes, waving off the advice.

He headed for the plate, which took some of the attention off me and the hysterical canine, but not all of it. I tried to remain calm, and just act as if none of this was happening. Which, after all, in some purist sense, might be true. This was hardly the caliber of breaking speed barriers and saving lives, I thought resentfully. So much for Al's theory, or Ziggy's theory – or whoever the hell's theory – that all this ridiculous leaping about might serve some greater cause. What greater cause would be served as a minor league baseball player?

Pop finally got fed up with the barking mascot. He glared at me. 'Okay, Fox, that's enough,' he said. 'Do something.'

'Me?' I replied, 'why me?'

Pop gave me a look that said, 'I don't have time for this.' 'Because,' he said, 'he's your dog!'

'My . . .' I looked from Pop to the terrier and back again. Then I turned my head slowly, as the realization of what was happening dawned on me. He knew! That barking little sucker *knew* I wasn't really Fox. Of course he did – an animal wouldn't be fooled by anything as transparent as a physical switch. They had other senses working for them – I probably didn't smell right or something.

He kept yapping angrily, and I stared into his incensed little doggy eyes. He knew, all right, and he wasn't about to stop barking. Not until they all knew. I tried to think what to do for a crazy dog – throw cold water on it? Nah, that might just exacerbate this little monster.

Then I had one of those all-of-a-piece memories which seemed to crop up and carry advice with them. I remembered suddenly that stray dogs had been kind of common in the farm belt where I was raised. And I remembered, too, that one of the first things my father taught me about them – especially the wild ones – was how to face them down. After all, we humans are much, much bigger. All you had to do, I recalled, was look them straight in the eye and let them know who's really the boss.

I stood up slowly to emphasize my size, and locked my

eyes onto Jack's. If anything, the hysterical barking seemed to intensify. I felt my face flush, chagrined. Of course, I rationalized, it had been a long time since I had been a kid. Maybe dogs had gotten more sophisticated.

But I kept my stare on him, and all of a sudden, the trick seemed to work. The terrier yapped once or twice, then quieted completely. He cocked his head to one side, and I could have sworn that he gave me a strange look of enquiry.

Well, buddy, I told him silently, when I find out . . . maybe I'll clue you in. His expression got even more peculiar. He blinked at me, then seemed to shake his head. Suddenly, he laid back down and put his paws over his eyes. I was very relieved.

'That's the damndest thing I ever saw!' exclaimed Pepper.

From behind me, I heard one of the other players ask, 'How'd you teach him a trick like that, Foxy?'

As I turned to formulate an answer, I came face to face with Albert, looking natty in a Lakers' cap and jacket.

'Yah!' I jumped a foot back, startled. So that's what Jack had been staring at!

My reaction seemed to set off a mini-chain reaction. Two or three other players jumped in response to my peculiar action . . . and on the field, completely ignoring Pop's plea, Barnes swung at the first pitch, and cracked a line drive in to right field.

'Hey, hey!' Doug Ibold's voice boomed over the loudspeaker. 'Barnes lines a solid shot into right. Pace is chasing it into the corner and Barnes is rounding first. Here's the throw to second and . . . he's safe!'

I saw a few of my teammates blink in surprise.

'The Bombers get their second hit of the game, and it's a double!'

'It ain't over till it's over,' Al observed cogently.

I saw Barnes stand from his slide and dust himself off. The fans seemed to find it all very hard to believe. Their applause was slow and scattered. A few who had already been gathering up their things and starting to leave the park paused and looked back. Some of them actually sat down again.

In the dugout, the reaction was about as slow as the crowd's. The only one applauding was the chubby bat boy. And Al.

'Jeez,' Al said with disgust, 'no wonder these guys are in the toilet. They've got all the enthusiasm of a ten buck hooker.'

I tried without thinking to yank Al into the locker room where I wouldn't be overheard talking, but naturally, my hands went right through him. He gave me a look of pity.

'Come on,' I hissed.

'What? And miss the game?'

'Will you please just follow me?' I said, frustrated.

Pepper turned to look at me. 'I can't. I'm up after Matt.'

'Ah . . . right,' I said, trying to smile.

'Something wrong, Fox?' asked Pop.

'Ah . . . no! Ah . . . I'll be back in a minute, gotta . . .' I gestured towards the tunnel, '. . . you know.'

Pop eyed me curiously, then spit another stream of tobacco juice. He glanced around the dugout. 'Next son of a bitch who swings on the first pitch, I'm fining fifty bucks.'

I strolled casually into the dim tunnel. Behind me, I could hear Pop clapping, trying to pump the team up. 'Let's go, come on! Let's go!'

I headed for the locker room as if I knew where I was going, until I noticed that Al was nowhere to be seen. I turned and glanced around wildly, just as he emerged from the wall.

'Jesus!' I said. 'How many times do I have to tell you to stop doing that!'

'Sorry,' he shrugged. 'I forgot.'

I tried to gather my scattered thoughts. 'How'd you get here so fast, anyway?' I asked.

'It's been a week since you quantum leaped,' Al informed me.

'A week?' I frowned. 'Really? A minute ago I was in the hospital with Peg.'

'Maybe to you,' Al said calmly. 'We've been popping champagne for six days.' He grinned happily. 'It was a hell of a party, Sam. Gushie got so wasted he had Ziggy spitting out erotic print-outs. And you know Angela, that cute little redhead in coding? Well, she got so turned on . . .'

'Damn it!' I said angrily. 'No! I don't know Angela, or I don't remember Angela, and I don't care! I'm having a real identity crisis here, Al. One minute I'm Tom Stratton, then next I'm some third-rate ball player named Fox! Tell me what the hell . . .'

'Your name is Tim Fox,' Al informed me obligingly. 'Thirty-two-year old third baseman for the Waco Bombers. According to Ziggy, you hit four-fifteen in '61, and were called up to Chicago.'

'I was?' I said, impressed.

'Then you broke your leg sliding into third base, and were sent down to recover.' He paused and eyed me warily. 'That was five years ago.'

Without thinking, I whirled and raced through the doors to the locker room, jerking myself to an abrupt stop in front of a sink with a mirror. The man looking back at me looked nothing like me or Tom Stratton. He looked . . . like a sandy haired, red faced, average Joe. In a baseball uniform. 'Oh, jeez,' I said weakly. 'Not again.' I don't know why the physical changes seemed to get to me more than anything else that went along with leap-ing. Except, I reflected, risking my life. Although there certainly didn't seem to be any danger of that this time . . .

There was an unexpected roar from the crowd out-side, and I turned, to see Al gazing longingly in that direction; he quite obviously would have preferred being out there.

His question confirmed my thoughts. 'Can't we talk in the dugout?' he whined. 'I'm missing the game.'

'To hell with the game!' I snapped.

He raised an eyebrow. 'It's your last one in organized ball,' he warned me. 'In a couple of minutes, you're gonna fly out to center. The Bombers will finish the season in the cellar and you'll hang up your cleats.'

I stared at him uncomprehendingly. 'Then what?'

He shrugged. 'Then you open a Kentucky Fried Chicken franchise. Marry a girl named Sue and have two kids.'

'Kentucky Fried Chicken?' I echoed disbelievingly. Boy, had I been right when I had intuited that there was nothing crucial about *this* little time leap!

'Of course,' he amended, 'you won't be around long enough to do all that. Once we figure out what needs to be set right, we'll leap you out of here.'

'Uh-huh,' I said cynically, 'like fly the X-2, break Mach three and live?'

Al held up one hand placatingly. 'We were a little off there,' he admitted. 'But not completely. Ziggy didn't research deeply enough. It seems that originally not only did Tom Stratton die, but his wife went into premature labor and the baby was stillborn.'

'Jesus,' I said softly, almost scared to ask the logical next question. 'And now?'

'And now there's a happy ending, instead. Tom's alive

and Peg delivered a healthy little girl. Seven pounds, eight ounces.' He grinned at me. 'They named her Samantha, of all things. Go figure.'

'So . . .' I said.

'So . . . it looks as if someone wanted Tom and Samantha both to make it.'

'I guess so,' I said slowly, a bit overwhelmed by the thought of what I had done. Or helped do.

'Shh! Listen!' Al said, cocking his head to the wall mounted speaker which carried Doug Ibold's running commentary on the game.

'Runners on first and second, no outs. Count's two and oh. Here's the pitch . . . It's a ground ball to short . . . takes a bad hop over McCombie's head! One run is . . . going to score!'

Al and I listened intently. Maybe I would get a clue, I thought, as to why I was here.

'Matt's rounding third. He's heading for home. Here comes the throw from left . . .'

I could hear the crowd moan.

'He's out. One run scores. Pepper goes to second on the throw home and the Bombers trail five to one.'

I turned back to the mirror, still studying the unfamiliar face there.

'Come on, Sam,' Al said impatiently, 'Jackson's going to hit a home run with two on.'

The voice was right next to me, but there was nothing in the mirror.

'You're a vampire!' I exclaimed.

'What?' Al stared at me, then at the mirror. 'Oh, that – neurological holograms don't reflect, Sam.' He frowned. 'Obviously, when it comes to quantum physics, you're still a mental slug this time around. Anyway, let's talk about this later – I hate missing the game.'

'But you know how it's going to end!' I said.

'I knew how it was going to end when I took Angela into the filing room, too. I still went.'

I chose to ignore that. 'Why didn't I leap all the way?' I demanded.

'Ten years in a blink ain't bad, pal,' Al said. 'A couple more like this one, you'll be home.' He paused and listened to the excited roar of the crowd. 'Oh, jeez, Sam! I missed the home run!'

'How many more of these leaps before I'm home?' I persisted.

'We're not exactly . . . sure,' Al said.

'You're hedging!' I accused him. When he didn't bother to deny it, I continued. 'In other words, I could be bouncing around like this forever!'

'Of course you couldn't,' Al said pragmatically. 'Nobody lives forever.'

'Oh, and am I supposed to find that comforting?' I steamed.

Doug Ibold's voice of Waco broke into our little altercation with a newfound excitement. 'Jackson's hit a towering smash over the Schneck and Schneck billboard in center field, and the Bombers have just pulled within a run!'

'Okay,' I said. 'I want this straight, Al. What do I have to do to put it right this time?'

'I don't know,' he said, shaking his head.

'You mean you're not sure,' I corrected him.

Al sighed. 'When you didn't leap all the way back, Ziggy got depressed.'

'Depressed?! He's a *computer*!'

'With a very big ego,' Al reminded me. 'To tell you the truth, Sam,' he said confidentially, 'I think he does have some ideas about what you have to do, but he's afraid to print them out in case he's wrong.'

That was the stupidest thing I had heard yet. The

solution was perfectly obvious to me. 'Just force him,' I said.

Al laughed. 'How?'

I thought about it for a moment. 'Threaten to pull his damned plug!'

Al looked at me sadly. 'He's self-energized, Sam.'

'And whose bright idea was *that*?' I asked, seething.

'Yours,' Al said mildly.

I stared at him blankly. 'What?'

Al seemed to wrestle with his conscience for a minute. 'Quantum Leap is your project, Sam.'

'Mine?' I echoed.

'Yes, yours. You're the genius behind it. Or, you were, anyway.'

'No,' I said, shaking my head, 'that can't be right. I'm a medical doctor. I found that out when Peg . . .'

'You hold six advanced degrees,' Al told me. 'Medicine is only one of them.'

'Oh.' I was at a loss for words.

'Your special gift *was* quantum physics – God knows where that little talent has disappeared to. *Time* magazine called you the new Einstein. The truth is . . .' he paused and stared at me meaningfully, 'you're the only one who can figure out how to get you back.'

I slumped back against the mirror. 'And I can't even remember my name,' I said.

Al reached out as if to touch me, realized he couldn't. He looked at me compassionately, then walked towards the tunnel, pausing by the pay phone. 'It's Beckett,' he said softly. 'Sam Beckett.'

CHAPTER EIGHTEEN

Then Al was gone. I stared at the spot where he had stood and repeated silently to myself, 'Sam Beckett. Sam. Beckett.' Me. I had a name. I also, it occurred to me, either had a set of parents with a strange sense of humor, or some kind of impeccable literary lineage. Now where had *that* idea come from?

There was no time to think about it. I was too stunned by the simple fact of knowing my name. I thought, my . . . *parents*. I had parents, and this was 1966, ten years later than my incarnation as Tom Stratton, but still . . . That meant they were both still alive. As if drawn by a magnet, I walked slowly over to the pay phone on the wall and stared fixedly at it.

I reached into my uniform pockets for change, but they were empty. That was hardly going to stop me, not at this point; I whirled around to the wall mounted lockers, and began to go through their contents. Pin-ups, photos of girl friends, kids, wives. An Afro comb. A Nehru jacket. Rubbers. No change!

'Ah . . .' I heard someone clear his throat tentatively, and I spun around and saw the chubby young batboy staring nervously at me. He had obviously seen what I was doing, and had no idea how to handle the situation.

'What!' I snapped.

He backed off into the hallway. 'You're on deck,' he squeaked.

'I need some change,' I said desperately. 'Do you have any?'

'Oh,' he said, relieved. 'Sure.' He trotted over to a battered foot locker and pulled out a jar of dimes and nickels. 'Help yourself, Mr. Fox,' he said.

'Thanks, kid, this one just can't wait.' I winked, allowing him to think that this was going to be a heavy-breathing conversation that demanded privacy. He blushed and retreated.

On deck, hell. This was a chance to do it. To talk to my father, to go back in time. It was the perfect fantasy.

I picked up the receiver and deposited a handful of change. 'Operator,' I said firmly, 'I'd like long distance please. Indiana.' I waited a moment while she connected me to long distance, then heard a new voice on the line.

'Indiana Long Distance, may I help you?'

'In Elk Ridge,' I said, 'do you have a number for a Beckett? A . . . John!' I remembered. 'John Beckett?'

I heard the sound of pages being riffled – this was truly pre-computer – 'Yes, sir,' she said, 'I'll connect you.'

'Thanks.' That's when I began to get really nervous. But there wasn't any time to think about how I was going to approach this delicate matter, what I was going to say, how I could explain myself, because after two rings, a man's voice answered. It was my father's voice, and hearing it set off an electrical shock-like feeling up and down my spine.

'Dad?' I said, my voice crackling with tension, or emotion, or both.

'What?' the man said, startled. 'I'm sorry, what did you say?'

'Ah . . .' I had already run out of words – how could I tell him who was calling?

'Hello!' His voice grew a little louder, more impatient. 'Hello!' he repeated. 'Whoever you are, I don't have time for this kind of tomfoolery . . .'

I knew he was about to disconnect. 'Don't hang

up!' I said desperately. 'Please.'

There was a pause. 'Who *is* this?' he asked.

It was so hard to believe that I was actually hearing his voice. I felt my throat tighten, but I had to go on – I couldn't let him get away. I said the first thing that popped into my head. 'I'm a Beckett!' I paused to collect my scrambled feelings, and a faint memory echoed through my head, a memory of distant relatives. 'Ah . . . my father and your father are related!'

'How?' Dad asked, suspicion and curiosity mingling in his gruff voice.

'Ah . . . brothers!' I remembered it now. 'I'm Tom's son.'

Dad paused, then he spoke, his voice surprised but friendly. 'Tom's son! My God! He moved to Australia when I was just a kid.' Then he laughed. 'Listen to me, telling you what your own father did!'

'Oh, that's all right,' I said weakly. Anything to keep him talking.

'What's your name?'

'Sam,' I replied without thinking.

'Well, I'll be darned!' Dad said happily. 'I've got a boy named Sam, too.'

'How about that?' I asked.

'You don't sound Australian, Sam.'

'Oh, I . . . travel a lot,' I improvised hastily.

'Are you some kind of salesman?' he asked dubiously.

'Oh, no . . . well.' I paused and pretended to cough. 'I represent a firm, but it's not really sales. And . . . I went to school in the States for a while. That's why the accent isn't . . . uh . . .'

'How's your dad?' my father asked, obviously trying to make me – his tongue-tied kin – feel more relaxed. 'I haven't heard anything about that branch of the family in years.'

I tried desperately to remember back, and took a flyer that my great Uncle Tom was still alive in 1966. What the hell? I thought. 'Fine,' I said firmly. 'We're all fine.' Then I added tentatively, 'Ah, the reason I'm calling is, I, uh, just wanted to hear your . . . a family voice. You know how it is – sometimes I really miss them.'

'I'm sure you do, Sam,' he said understandingly. 'Family's so important, and yours is so far away.'

If you only knew, I thought, and felt tears well up suddenly in my eyes. 'Yes,' I said, 'it is. I'd like . . .' I tried to control my voice, 'I'd like to go home and see them, but it just doesn't look as if it's possible. Not now. And even if it was, well . . . I just couldn't. There's too much at stake . . . here.' My voice trailed off.

'You mean, with your business and all?' my dad asked.

'Maybe,' I said quietly. 'Maybe for them, maybe for someone else, someone I haven't even met, yet.' I forced a little laugh. 'I guess this all sounds pretty crazy to you, but I really can't explain. Especially over the phone.' I felt as if I was babbling, but anything to keep him on the line, to keep hearing that kind, gruff voice from my long-ago past.

'Well,' Dad said thoughtfully, 'if you've got any time on your hands at all, why don't you come on up here for a visit? I'd love to see you . . .'

'I'd love to see you, too,' I said sadly, knowing as I said it that it was an impossibility.

'We've got plenty of room – we've got a farm.'

I nodded, feeling tears in my eyes.

'. . . and Mom's the best cook around. She bakes up the best peach cobbler in Lincoln county . . .'

I felt the tears spill over and course down my face as he continued with words I knew by heart, words I mouthed along with him.

'. . . maybe even the whole state.'

'That sounds great,' I said, choking the words out. 'I'd really like that – I'm just not sure when I can make it.'

'Well, we're not going anywhere, son.' I heard another voice behind him, and heard Dad say in a muffled tone, 'Be there in a minute, Sam. It's your . . . second, no third cousin, I guess. My Uncle Tom's boy, from Australia.' He paused. 'No, he's here.' Then his voice came back on the line. 'That was *my* Sam,' he said. There was real pleasure in his voice.

'Uh-huh,' I said, my voice cracking. He's proud of me, I thought. I could hear it in the way he talked to Sam. Me.

'Listen, Sam,' my father's voice was gentle, 'I barely remember your dad, and you and I've never met, but I can tell by talking to you that you've got some problems you're trying to work out.'

'I do,' I said softly.

'Well, it's simple advice, but just remember this, son: you're a Beckett. And whatever a Beckett faces, he faces with courage and faith in the Lord. As long as you do that, Sam, you can't make a wrong decision.'

'Thank you, sir,' I whispered.

'Goodbye, Sam,' he said.

'Goodbye,' I replied, and heard the click of his receiver. I stood there, listening, until the dead space became a dial tone, then I hung up.

I looked up at the dingy cracked ceiling of the locker room. 'Thank you,' I whispered to whatever or whoever was above me. Then I splashed some cold water on my tear-stained face, gave my cap a tug, and headed resolutely back out to the dugout. I still didn't know why I was here, but I had to believe, I *did* believe, it was for some good reason.

I made my way into the dugout just in time to see the batter make a determined swing at a curve ball, and crack a linedrive along the third baseline. It ricocheted off the bag and slid down the fence, and the fans, roused from their former lethargy by the unexpected and dramatic turn in the game, went nuts – cheering, whistling, hooting, while the batter raced around first and went non-stop on to second before the throw reached it.

'I don't believe it!' Doug Ibold's voice went up an octave. 'Clyde's hit a stand-up double! The tying run is on second, and the potential winning run is coming to bat! Talk about a wild turnaround, folks, this is history you're seeing tonight!'

'That's you, Sam.' It was Al's voice, and I saw him peering seriously from me to the field and back again.

All of a sudden, I had an overwhelming feeling of happiness. Maybe this quantum leaping around was all right, I thought, maybe it really did serve some purpose, set some things right. Maybe I could make the world a better place.

'Thanks, Al,' I whispered. He looked at me as if I was crazy.

The team, my teammates, that is, had also woken up from their season-long stupor. They clapped and yelled words of encouragement to me as I made my way through the dugout. Even Jack the dog seemed up for this, running in circles and barking happily.

'Go get 'em,' I heard Al say.

As I climbed the steps to the field, Pop put his hand on my shoulder. 'Fox,' he said. He stopped for a minute and seemed almost embarrassed. Then he went on. 'Remember, Fox, this is *my* last year, too. I . . . don't want to go out in the cellar.'

And then I understood that maybe *this* was what needed to be put right. Maybe this time, it was all as simple as granting a wish to a good man who had devoted his life to a good game. Why not? I nodded purposefully, and stepped onto the field to the roars of the crowd.

'Give me one with a four-bagger in it, son.'

The bat-boy nodded happily and scurried off to the bat rack.

'You've got to be kidding,' Al said disbelievingly. 'You know who that is on the mound?'

I squinted out into the lights. From where I stood, the pitcher looked an awful lot like a very young Tom Seaver.

I nodded and shrugged. 'Yeah. So?'

The bat-boy ran back and handed me a bat. I hefted it – it felt good, and I grinned at the boy.

'I got the play by play from Ziggy,' Al said mournfully. 'You're gonna fly out to center.'

I swung the bat a few times. '*Fox* flied out to center,' I told Al. 'I'm not Fox.'

I strode over to the mound. From behind me, I heard Al say, 'You're not Roy Hobbs, either.'

As I reached the plate, there was a sudden crack! in the sky. A streak of lightning split the dark night, followed by a sharp clap of thunder. I nodded. 'Got it,' I said softly.

Ibold's voice came over the loudspeaker. 'Fox, representing the winning run, steps to the plate. A switch hitter . . .'

Whew, I thought; I had automatically stepped up to swing lefty.

'. . . Fox has twenty-eight home runs this year. Twelve of them batting left handed.'

I rotated my shoulders, hunkered down, and . . . the first pitch zipped by me so fast I didn't even get the bat off my shoulder! This was going to be a little more difficult than I thought.

'He takes a fast ball down the middle for strike one.'

Okay, I told myself, this is it. I dug in and concentrated. I saw the pitcher give a series of signals, then wind up and then . . . the second ball went whistling past me.

'Stee-rike!' I heard the umpire yell over the crowd's groans of disappointment. Out of the corner of my eye, I could see a few of the ones who had returned to their seats when the game looked as if it might turn around, begin to gather up their things again. Oh no you don't, I thought.

I stepped out of the box and re-gripped the bat. Al appeared at my side. 'That last one must have been over a hundred,' he observed.

'I'll get the next one,' I swore.

The umpire looked over at me. 'You call time, Fox?'

I shook my head. 'No. Play ball.' And I stepped back into the box.

I could just hear Ibold winding up his last commercial spiel. 'Fox steps back into the box. He digs in. Behind oh-and-two on the count, he looks determined not to let another pitch go by . . .'

I stared hard at the pitcher, locking eyes with him, trying to psych him out. He went into a wind up. Above us, lightning flashed again and the crowd gasped.

This time I saw the ball; it must have been as fast, no, faster than the others, but I let loose with a mighty swing and . . . missed. I sagged in defeat, the bat swinging at my side. How was I going to face Pop?

But just at the moment it looked as if it was all over, I suddenly heard Al bellowing at the top of his lungs. 'Turn around, Sam, turn around!'

I whirled and saw the ball skip away into the dirt behind home plate.

'Go!' Al screamed. 'Go!'

Jesus, I realized in a blinding flash, the catcher had dropped the third strike! I could run! I dropped the bat and raced for first. Glancing wildly behind me, I could see a comedy of errors unfold. The catcher chased down the ball and one-handed it to first to try to strike me out. But the ball went wild, right over the first baseman's outstretched hand into right field.

'Wow!' I whispered, and then I headed for second . . .

'Go, go!' I could still hear Al, as I saw Clyde ahead of me, rounding home plate for the tying run. Here we go, Pop! I thought, skating lightly over second and pounding for third. I made it to third about one tenth of a second before the right fielder's throw would have gotten there *if* he had thrown straight. But he didn't! Luck continued to be on my side as the ball bounced right past the third baseman's diving stretch, and, my heart thundering in my chest, I headed for home. This was it!

'Go, Sam, go!' I heard Al screaming over the noise of the crowd.

My heart felt as if it was going to burst through my chest. Then things seemed to happen in slow motion. Peripherally, I could see the crowd leaping up and down as one, I could hear them screaming for me to score. I could see the entire team, Pop and the dog Jack, emptying out of the dugout and onto the field. Above all, I could still hear Al cheering me on.

As I sprinted for home, I could see Al, too; he was jumping up and down, waving his arms to indicate danger, and I knew that someone had gotten to that ball and I was racing with the clock to make this winning run. I had to do it, I had to!

I dove automatically for the plate, head first, and with my face in the dirt, I went into what seemed like an interminable slide, dust rising in clouds around me, obscuring my vision. As my arms scraped through the blinding dirt of that last endless yard, I heard thunder and lightning above me, and a strange roaring sound begin. As if from behind a wavy, distant glass, I saw the ball nearing the hand of the catcher, nearer and nearer, as I, too, got nearer and nearer . . .

And then all I could see was the umpire, his arms stretched up to the sky as he signalled my triumph! I'd made it!

Still prone in the dirt, I threw my head up and prepared for a Hallelujah! which would reach to heaven, when all of a sudden, there was nothing around me but black, rushing space. No field, no umpire, no Pop, no Al . . . just a cracking sound, a trembling, shaking feeling, and then, just rolling darkness.

Oh, God, I thought, here we go again . . .

THE END